"One achieves a kind of serenity when delving into this book. I find that eccentrics like Jung are needed in literature." —ACHIM STANISLAWSKI

Author & Translator Biographies

JUNG YOUNG MOON was born in Hamyang, South Gyeongsang Province, South Korea in 1965. He graduated from Seoul National University with a degree in psychology. He made his literary début in 1996 with the novel *A Man Who Barely Exists*. Jung is also an accomplished translator who has translated more than forty books from English into Korean, including works by John Fowles, Raymond Carver, and Germaine Greer. In 1999 he won the 12th Dongseo Literary Award with his collection of short stories, A Chain of Dark Tales. In 2005 Jung was invited to participate in the University of Iowa's International Writing Program, and in 2010 the University of California at Berkeley's Center for Korean Study invited him to participate in a three-month-long residency program. In 2012 he won the Han Moo-suk Literary Award, the Dong-in Literary Award, and the Daesan Literary Award for his novel *A Contrived World*, forthcoming from Dalkey Archive, who also published his short story collection *A Most Ambiguous Sunday and Other Stories* in 2014. His works have been translated into numerous languages, and he is widely read in France and Germany, where he enjoys great critical acclaim and popular appeal.

YEWON JUNG was born in Seoul, and moved to the US at the age of 12. She received a BA in English from Brigham Young University, and an MA from the Graduate School of Interpretation and Translation at Hankuk University of Foreign Studies.

VASELINE
BUDDHA

—

Jung Young Moon

TRANSLATED FROM THE KOREAN BY
YEWON JUNG

DEEP VELLUM PUBLISHING

DALLAS, TEXAS

Deep Vellum Publishing
3000 Commerce St., Dallas, Texas 75226
deepvellum.org · @deepvellum

Deep Vellum Publishing is a 501c3
nonprofit literary arts organization founded in 2013.

ISBN: 978-1-941920-34-3 (paperback) · 978-1-941920-35-0 (ebook)
LIBRARY OF CONGRESS CONTROL NUMBER: 2015960723
—

Vaseline Buddha *is published under the support of*
Literature Translation Institute of Korea (LTI Korea).

LTI Korea
Literature Translation Institute of Korea
—

Cover design & typesetting by Anna Zylicz · annazylicz.com

Text set in Bembo, a typeface modeled on typefaces cut by Francesco Griffo
for Aldo Manuzio's printing of *De Aetna* in 1495 in Venice.

Distributed by Consortium Book Sales & Distribution.

Printed in the United States of America on acid-free paper.

Vaseline Buddha

One day, when the night was giving way to dawn and everything was still immersed in darkness, I sat on a windowsill in the house I lived in, unable to sleep, thinking vaguely that I would write a story. I didn't know at all where or what the story, if it could be called a story, would head toward, nor did I want to know in advance, and for the time being, there was nothing that told me where to go or what to do. So for the time being I was right to think that it could turn into a story, but it was possible that it wouldn't turn into a story at all.

Anyhow, something happened a little before I began thinking such things, something so trivial that you could hardly say that anything had happened at all; I heard a very small sound coming from outside the kitchen window, and straining my ears for the sound for a moment, I thought it was the sound of raindrops, but it didn't continue at regular intervals like the sound of raindrops. After a little while, I went to the bedroom windowsill and looked out the window through the curtains but it wasn't raining, and with a certain thought in mind I went to the kitchen where the sound had come from, hid myself behind a wall, and saw someone climbing up toward my bedroom window. It seemed that he was climbing up the gas pipes, and he looked like a moving shadow.

It was an astonishing sight but I didn't cry out because I felt as if I were dreaming. He was taking great care not to wake the person inside, whom he thought was sound asleep.

After a little while, I saw him trying to open the window, and I stuck my face out quietly so as not to startle him, but at that moment he saw my face and was so startled that he fell to the ground. I hadn't had the slightest intention of startling him, so I felt terrible, as if I had made him fall even though I hadn't, and above all, I wondered if he was all right, having fallen to the ground. He picked himself up at once, but was limping slightly, probably with a strained ankle, and went across the small yard and tried to climb over the wall which wasn't so high, which didn't look easy, either. I wished I could help him climb over the wall by giving him a leg-up. After several attempts, he finally clambered up the wall and disappeared into the darkness after throwing one last look in my direction, but I couldn't tell if he looked at me with reproach as he disappeared into the darkness.

Keeping an eye on the spot from which he had disappeared, I wondered for a moment as to what he was. I concluded that he wasn't a robber since I didn't see a weapon in his hand nor a weapon he could have dropped. Nobody but a thief, then, would pay me a quiet visit through my window at that hour. I thought about the great misfortune of the thief who had surely been after something in my house where there was nearly nothing worth taking, if not after me. Everything requires a certain amount of luck, especially in his line of work, but he hadn't had any luck at all. I smiled, thinking about his circumstances as well as my own, not much better than his. Or I should say, I smiled, aware of the smile that spread across my face, thinking that the man who had appeared out of darkness and disappeared back into the darkness was like a beaver that came out of water in the dark of the night and disappeared back into the water.

And although I wasn't in a position to worry about his circumstances I hoped that the man, who had elicited feelings of sadness in me about his misfortune as well as a gentle smile from me for the first time in a while, and who hadn't seemed fit to be a thief and had perhaps had his first experience as a thief that day, would have some luck in the future, and that he, having perhaps chosen a night job because he had trouble sleeping at night as I did, wouldn't be too angry about his experience that early morning, and would be able to smile, feeling somewhat sheepish.

And I thought I saw in the darkness three cats walking with some distance among themselves, on the wall over which the thief had disappeared, but I wasn't sure if I actually saw them, or if I was deluded, or if I was imagining them. Yet it seemed that the cats were taking the route they always took and that nothing had happened in the meantime.

I went back to bed and lay down, and suddenly wondered who was at fault for the fall of the thief, who fell because of me although I didn't throw him down, but who wouldn't have fallen if it hadn't been for me, and as I often did when it wasn't clear who was at fault, I thought I was a little more at fault. But it seemed that no one was at fault for the fall, and I thought that there were things in the world for which no one was at fault, and things that couldn't really be called a fault, and although I thought that the conclusion wasn't adequate, that was the conclusion I wanted to draw.

And I also thought that all he'd tried to do was to obtain something he didn't have, which was quite natural. And maybe it was a good thing that he went away like that, for it also occurred to me that otherwise a strange confrontation might have taken place between the man who came into the house and me in my underwear, leading to unpleasant acts or conversations.

And after a while, thoughts regarding what had just happened faded away, and it seemed that nothing had happened, that it had all been a dream. But as I mused on what had just happened, I gradually became almost glad that he'd come like that, because for some time I'd been staying cooped up at home without seeing anyone. Before he paid me a visit that night I'd been feeling so alone, not having spoken a word to anyone for days, and yet looking at the curtains flapping now and then in the open window and thinking that I wouldn't go outside unless a gigantic sailboat, with a full load and the sails taut with wind, entered through the window. I had no apparent reason for not going outside, but I had to rationalize my not going outside, even if it meant making up a reason like that. It seemed that something left behind by the man who hadn't taken anything from me was hovering around me, having faded without disappearing, like a lingering impression, although it wasn't a lingering impression. The thief, who had come to my place to accomplish something but failed in the end, hadn't done anything to me or left anything for me, but it seemed that something he'd left behind had been left for me.

For some time, I'd been in a constant state of lethargy—so constant that it was amazing when I thought about it—and had been unable to do anything, and hadn't been doing anything. But an urge to write was awakened within me as if the thief, who went away without actually doing anything, had done something to me, had provoked me in some way as I thought about him, and thoughts began to squirm in my mind, like a stiffened body attempting some difficult movements. The vague stories that I'd tried to write down but had escaped me began to blossom little by little, and I wanted to give them a vague form that suited them. And I thought that the story I was to write could be like the experience I'd just had, which was really nothing at all, that I could make it that way, and thus write about intangible things, or about making things intangible.

Now there's no sound coming from outside. I stare for a long time at the darkness outside from which no sound comes, or perhaps I just can't hear the sound that's coming. And staring at the darkness outside from within the utter darkness in the house, I think that thoughts on darkness could shed a certain light on what I'm about to write, to make all that's obscure even more obscure, and if not, make it remain as obscure as it is, that what I'm about to write could turn into something that resembles certain shapes created by light and darkness, and that, although this sounds strange, there are things in life that can be revealed by shedding darkness, not light, on them. And thinking into the morning, I think that perhaps what I'm about to write will be about thoughts on my own thoughts themselves, or things that occur in my thoughts, or various thoughts that come out of thoughts and burrow into other thoughts or disappear, a sort of a daily record of thoughts, something that traps everything in certain thoughts and reveals itself through certain words or sentences.

I think it was one fine morning around the beginning of summer, when I heard a kitten, which seemed to have been abandoned by its mother, crying until it was exhausted, trapped in pumpkin vines in a little patch of ground in the garden that belonged to the strange old couple whose house I was renting, that I began to have more concrete but still vague thoughts about what I'm writing. The meow of the kitten was similar to the sound that comes when you squeeze the belly of certain dolls, certain baby dolls in particular, but the kitten, which never came out of the thick pumpkin vines, no longer made a sound, probably dead.

I felt a peculiar excitement as I pictured the kitten, though I couldn't see it, trembling in fear among the pumpkin vines which must have seemed to the kitten like a jungle without an exit, so I wound up a music box that was on the table by the windowsill, and as I listened to the short melody, which sounded sad because it was in a minor key—I have several music boxes, and I like to play two or three of them at the same time and listen to the sound—I thought that what I wanted to write was becoming a little more concrete. But actually, it wasn't concrete at all, and all I could think was that I could think about entering a story in which you'd get lost, like setting foot in a world from which you can't extricate yourself.

Or perhaps this story had its beginning, insignificant as it was, during my stay in a small town in France very long ago, when I was struggling through an unbearable boredom that was, in its own way, desperate. The little town where I stayed for several months was an extremely boring place where the typical French bourgeoisie lived, with royal villas of the French royal family of the past nearby, and I usually managed to wake up only in the afternoon because of the wine I'd drunk through the night, and spent my time taking a walk in a park or sitting still on a bench in the park, where there were many old people, as there are in any park in Europe, sitting still on the benches and staring fixedly at something. I couldn't tell what the people, who seemed to be sitting there with all the strength they could muster, almost desperately, but were in reality barely managing to sit there, exhausted, and whom I felt exhausted just watching and yet couldn't easily take my eyes off, were watching, or not watching, or if they were watching something without seeing it, or imagining something they couldn't see to be something else, but for a long time, I'd watch the people sitting on the benches, who had become one with the benches, and the benches that had become one with them, and the benches that were left on their own because the people left at a certain hour, the benches, to speak from the position of the benches themselves, that were allowed to be left on their own because the people had left.

And at a certain hour of the day, I'd see an old woman walk over, dragging her feet, to the bench in the park—the park was in a quiet area on a residential street where no tourists came— where she always sat, which other people left empty for her or avoided sitting on for that reason, and sit there knitting a little sweater for someone. She knitted so slowly that it would've been impossible to do so on purpose, and it seemed that she was trying to postpone the end of her life, or end of the world, which didn't have that much to do with herself, which would come the moment the sweater was finished, even though she had no real reason for doing so.

I would sit across the bench where she was sitting, eating little pieces of a baguette I'd brought, either the part that was left over after I gave some to the pigeons or the part that was left over after I ate some and then gave to the pigeons, or the part that was left over after we ate some together, or slowly eat a boiled potato, peeling the skin off bit by tiny bit, or eat corn, one grain at a time, pulling the grains out with meticulous care—when I did, I felt as if I were a jeweler setting tiny stones in a piece of jewelry—and from time to time, she, too, would lift her eyes, and without any change in her expression, look in my direction, as if to see how fast or slow I was doing something. I wasn't sure if she could see me, sitting a little distance apart, and was thus able to tell what I was doing, or if she were merely turning her eyes to a form that she presumed to be human but didn't look human.

I always went to the park unless I was too depressed or couldn't get up because I was hung over from drinking too much, and took part in that strange game, perhaps a game I alone imagined we were playing, and each time, I imagined one of us winning or losing or the two of us drawing a tie, and always, it was the old woman whom I rooted for in my heart, and who thus won in my heart.

One day in late autumn that year, I saw her for the last time, attaching an arm to the body of the sweater, after which she no longer came out to the park, and I never found out if she had died without finishing the sweater, or quit just before she finished because she got tired of knitting the sweater, or became angry that she had spent so long knitting the sweater and burned it or unraveled it, or stopped coming outside just because it was cold. Nor did I find out if she really had someone for whom to knit a sweater. The only thing I'd seen by her side, in fact, was her dog.

The old woman had a little dog that took after her in many ways. The dog sat motionless before her while she sat knitting, and it had to sit motionless like that. The old woman didn't like it when the dog moved or wandered around. She could have let the dog roam about freely, without going far, within a range where her short vision reached, but she didn't. But the dog, not having an easy time staying still, just like humans—it's difficult for both humans and dogs to stay still, and probably more difficult than anything else—did all it could to move around while studying her face, but the woman did all she could to make the dog stay still, as if she bore a grudge against it. If the dog actually made to move, even slightly or sometimes even before the dog actually moved, the old woman would stop knitting and glare at the dog, and when she did, the dog became frightened and sat motionless like a well-trained dog. From time to time, when other dogs passed before the old woman and the dog, the dog, wanting to express how it felt to the other dogs, which were of its own kind, but knowing it wasn't allowed to do so, expressed unutterable pain, for all it could express was unutterable pain. The dog opened its mouth as if to say something but didn't bark or anything, and expressed its unutterable pain by digging in the ground with its paws, which was far from enough.

I didn't know how the old woman had trained the dog to stay

so still, or if she was punishing the dog in some way by making it stay still, or expressing love in her own way. In any case, the old woman never neglected to watch the dog even as she knitted, as if she were more concerned with the dog moving than her knitting. Maybe she was knitting a sweater for the dog, and was making the dog wait without moving an inch, at least until the sweater was finished.

Curiously, the dog sometimes stood in place, shaking all over, and it seemed in those moments that it was in some kind of a convulsion. Maybe it was because the dog had remained still for too long, or maybe it was its own way of moving around. Once in such a state, it shook continuously for about half an hour, and nothing could be done about it. The old woman—she was a horrid old woman—would at last glance at the dog as if to make sure that it was her dog and no one else's. The dog was mesmerized by whatever it was that was making it shake, I was mesmerized in watching the dog that was mesmerized by something, and the old woman was mesmerized in her knitting, and it seemed in those moments that we were all mesmerized, afflicted by something that mesmerized us while afflicting us.

The dog, however, wasn't actually a dog accompanying the old woman with whom I spent afternoons in a park in France. The dog belonged to another woman, middle-aged, who came to the park at a certain hour. The reason why I said that the dog that belonged to the middle-aged woman was the old woman's—it was the middle-aged woman who made the dog stay still, and it was she who was horrid—was because by putting a leash in the old woman's hand, I could picture a scene in which the woman and the dog walked across the park side by side on their way home, looking lonely, and funny at the same time. In any case, the fact that I'm talking about an old woman knitting in a park in France, and telling an anecdote about a dog that was mesmerized by something, whatever it was, may suggest that this story will be about certain thoughts that mesmerize and afflict me.

When put this way, what I'm saying may sound like the truth, but this story, at least the part about the dog, isn't true. I actually saw the dog recently in the garden of a café near my place. The dog came into the story somewhat arbitrarily because I put it in a past story in my memory. Anyway, the dog does go into convulsions from time to time, and usually seems stricken with fear. When someone approaches the doghouse, the dog, which is always in the doghouse, begins to bark loudly at once, at first out of gladness because it's always alone, but while barking out of gladness it changes its mind instantly, realizing that it's afraid of something, and begins to bark in a fearful voice, no longer glad, but no one can tell what it is that makes the dog tremble in fear.

Actually, the story about the old woman itself isn't true. I'm making up new stories by mixing up my memories and thoughts, and linking together things that have nothing to do with each other. There actually were old women who came to the park and sat on benches for a long time, but there wasn't one who spent all day there. (What I'm saying is that I'll be telling a story in which gazes fixed on certain things, and memories and thoughts, are jumbled together.) When I take my eyes off the people who come to the little old park, I see myself sitting blankly on a bench, afflicted by a number of thoughts. I was able to leave the city, where I spent my time for some obscure reason, after going to the riverside one winter day and coming across a large, dolphin-shaped tube floating down the river—many things floated down the river in my memory, because ever since I was little, I always liked to idly watch the river—and while slowly walking by the riverside with the tube alongside me—I pictured in my mind a clumsy-looking band slowly marching along the riverside while playing a slow tune—saw it finally disappear from my view.

I spent the summer and autumn that year lying among the shrubs on the sandy plain along the river, looking at the river and feeling that my life had expired or I had entered a thoroughly wrong path. No, I thought I had yet to go down many more wrong paths in order to enter a thoroughly wrong path.

At any rate, the dolphin-shaped tube I saw, which could have been thrown out by a father who was angry at his child, or by a child who was disappointed in, or felt betrayed by, his father, or by someone in the family who was angry for some reason or angry at nothing other than the tube itself, which caught the person's eye at that moment, or which was floating down the winter river for some other obscure reason, did not come to me as some kind of a revelation, because to the end, I did not let the tube, which hadn't come to me as a revelation from the beginning, come to me as a revelation. Nevertheless, the dolphin tube gave me enough motivation to leave the city—perhaps I took the tube, which hadn't come to me as a revelation, as some kind of a suggestion—which was perhaps because I was occupied with thoughts about the sentence, "Colorless green ideas sleep furiously," composed by a linguist, which I'd read around that time but hadn't understood the precise meaning of, and vaguely thought, when the tube had floated down the meandering river and could no longer be seen, that I may end up writing something, something about the difficulty of existence, the difficulty of talking about the difficulty of existence, the double difficulty of it, and that it would begin with me leaving the city. (How easy is it, though, for such words to be without truth? Thinking about the colossal gap between truth and falsehood, the gray area that can't be named, and thinking that the gap must be filled by fabrication, as inadequate as it is, I think that this story, too, will consist mostly of such fabrication.)

Watching the dolphin on the river, which was disappearing from my view, I regretted that I wasn't wearing a black fedora, because it seemed that the act of taking it off, hanging it on a branch of a bare tree on the winter riverside, then leaving the spot—I have a habit of calling up specific objects when I can't carry on with abstract thoughts—would serve as a gracious farewell to the dolphin that could no longer be seen, and would perhaps, if lucky, reach the sea, which would suit it better, and float around among real dolphins, triggering their curiosity, as well as a farewell to a certain period in my life. Furthermore, I liked to think, although it wasn't true, that the dolphin tube I saw floating down a winter river made for me a decision that I myself had difficulty making, and that the course of my life had thus changed slightly, indeed ever so slightly, because it was a good thing, at least in my mind, for the course of my life to change, be it slightly, by a dolphin tube I happened to see floating down a river one day, or by something that had nothing to do with me, like the tube, something that was almost nothing at all.

I myself couldn't say whether or not this was true. But there are thoughts that, despite having occurred in the mind, become more real in the mind than things that have actually taken place, which is the case for the thoughts above. And the thoughts may be telling me that I already know that what I'm writing will be about things that tell me nothing. And talking about things that tell you nothing is probably the same as thinking about things that remain obscure to the end.

In effect, what I really want to talk about is something that's nothing, or things you can't talk about. Although most of them are difficult to talk about, you can talk at least about the ways in which you can't talk about them, and how inexpressible they are, or how inexpressibly expressible they are, in which, perhaps, lies the ultimate something of speaking.

Or perhaps these words were conceived in my mind and had their beginning in the moment I felt severe dizziness as I watched a number of black birds, which had been sitting on a tree, suddenly soaring all at once into the darkening sky when I absently threw a rock while taking a walk in the woods near my house one evening.

(Between the moment when I'm writing a sentence and the moment when the thing spoken of in the sentence actually or fictionally took place, there's a space like a river that must be crossed by swimming, and I could be swept away by the current to a wrong place while crossing the river.)

At that moment, I thought that I could make certain motifs appear repeatedly in my story—you could say that that's the only idea I came up with while contemplating this story—while think- ing that I could write something about someone who constantly felt dizzy, and at the same time, thinking that I had witnessed in the past scenes similar to that of the birds soaring into the darkening sky and disappearing.

It's true, however, that around that time, I was thinking a lot about a species of parrot called kea that lives in the highlands of New Zealand, which I happened to read about in a newspaper article, but it's clear that the fact bears no direct relation to how I came to write this. . . But is it so clear?

Through the article, I found out that keas are birds that have feathers with a green tint, are bigger than ordinary parrots and intelligent enough to push or pull an object in a certain order so as to obtain food, are full of curiosity, and go through clothes and stuff people leave lying around, taking a short break while traveling, and take out the things in the pockets or just fly away with the clothes in their beaks, and have a cruel eating habit in which they alight mostly on sheep feeding on grass and make them die a slow, painful death, by delving into the sheep's bodies using their beaks and claws and eating the kidneys, but the paper did not carry a picture of the birds and I couldn't see what they looked like.

In reality the sheep may flee, or put up a struggle, at least, instead of having their kidneys ripped out by parrots while quietly grazing on grass, but in my imagination they are quietly grazing on grass even as their kidneys are being ripped out by the parrots. The feeling that sheep, which graze on grass incessantly to satisfy or appease a hunger that isn't easily satisfied or appeased, feel with the greatest intensity in their life is probably none other than hunger, and it must be their fate to feel constant hunger. (Some facts, though irrelevant to me, lead me to feel pain or think about pain just because they are facts, and the fact about the sheep in the highlands of New Zealand is among them.)

The sheep, unlike some monkeys that, looking very startled, cry out in a quite peculiar way, meaning, Watch out, eagles, when feeling threatened by eagles that prey on them, may think, The only way for us to beat those parrots is to flaunt our fearsome silence while having our kidneys ripped out, and this may serve as a clue in understanding the fearsome silence of sheep. And there's something humorous about another aspect of sheep in my mind, which is that they release methane, a greenhouse gas, as they quietly, and solemnly, burp. A cycle of revenge is created in which keas, which have lived in the highlands of New Zealand for a long time in my fantasy about sheep taking revenge on humans who have long been slaughtering them, by quietly and solemnly releasing methane, take revenge on sheep, brought by European immigrants, which have invaded their territory, and sheep take revenge on humans (this is one of the many notions I have of sheep), and humans take revenge on everything for no good reason (this seems very human to me). I imagine that herbivores that stuff themselves with things they shouldn't eat, things that are raised as livestock by humans, because humans force them to eat such things, are taking revenge now only by quietly burping and farting, but that they are quietly and solemnly preparing a great revenge which defies comparison to burps or farts, and that it'll come as a great catastrophe to humans someday. And this idea arises from the belief that it's unjust for humans to rule over this world thinking they can do whatever they please with this world.

Picturing parrots that are constantly after sheep kidneys and sheep that could lose their kidneys to parrots if they don't watch out, and which live together in their own kind of peace, though not at peace, I thought about the connection between things that are difficult to connect, and a performance by parrots and sheep held on the stage of the highlands of New Zealand seemed, to me at least, something more surreal than (or as surreal as) any surrealistic painting or film or play, and led me to think that I should like to include in this piece a surrealistic element, whose meaning I've reconsidered for a long time, and which is an important literary legacy, though neglected today, and also led me to think that I could make some other possible attempt by doing so, and that it could be one of the features of what I intended to write.

And now, momentarily lost in an unrealistic fantasy, I think that in order to see, understand, accept, and describe the reality of a moment, you need to make an effort to not see reality as it is, an effort at distortion, to see it from another angle, from another level, and in another way, and not merely evade it, and that there's a reality that can be reached only beyond realism. And I think that surrealism, with its obscure boundaries, lies not beyond realism, but could become undeniable reality within reality. It seems that I think somewhat lightly of realism—this could mean realism in a broad sense in some cases, and in others, a narrow sense—but it occurs to me, too, that there's something in realism that could be taken somewhat lightly. And I think about what an unrealistic world I live in, and that perhaps the world in which those unrealistic things come back to become my reality is the very place I can feel comfortable in. And I feel that the highlands of New Zealand I picture in my mind, at least where there are sheep having their kidneys ripped out by parrots, are an undeniable reality to me, though it seems like a surreal world, and that I undeniably exist before that undeniable surreality.

Perhaps I could add here a scene that has something to do with me seeing a flock of swallows that came flying from somewhere repeatedly swooping down, brushing against the surface of the water in the pool that no one entered because the water was too cold, and flying away as I lay reading one afternoon at the poolside at a hotel in a resort (I'd been in Nepal for several days at the time, but I was in a state in which I couldn't tell why I was there, and the fact that someone told me that he saw me die a terrible death in a foreign land in his dream, not long before I went to Nepal, had nothing to do with the trip. Actually, I had vaguely intended to go to Tibet or India, not Nepal, and vaguely thought before I went on the trip to Nepal that I wanted to see the yaks in the Himalayas where I could see snow-covered mountains right before my eyes—I'd seen on television how the yaks, full of suspicion, ate only the salt that their keepers fed them, even though salt was something that was essential for them, so I wanted to see for myself if that really was the case, and above all, I wanted to feed the yaks salt with my own hands, and told the people I met around that time that I was going to the Himalayas to see yaks, and it felt like the truth—but it wasn't to see yaks that I went to the Himalayas. But yaks were at a higher altitude than the altitude to which I climbed, and I ended up not seeing a single yak and had to come down from the Himalayas after getting an eyeful of nothing but donkeys. One of the things I realized while climbing the snow-covered mountains of the Himalayas was that you have to be more careful to not trip and fall over the donkey droppings that were scattered all over the road than to not fall down the cliff that was thousands of meters deep. Of course, you'd also have to be careful not to fall down the cliff that was thousands of meters deep by tripping over donkey droppings.) Several days earlier, standing before the impressive snow-covered mountains, over eight thousand meters high, I'd summed up my feelings about the mountains in the words, Here are some very, no, somewhat high mountains that are covered with snow, but so what? And the emotions that were stirred up by the snow-covered mountains became trapped in those words. Actually, the majestic view of the snow-covered mountains was decent at first, but then it wasn't as decent as it was at first, and then it was just so-so, and looking at them was similar to listening to a majestic but boring symphony that caught your ears when the performance began, but soon made you feel nothing at all.

But watching the swallows brushing against the water and soaring at the poolside reminded me of an experience I had in a little airplane flying precariously among snow-covered mountains over eight thousand meters high, and the swallows washed away all my regret for having come to Nepal. The old airplane of a small airline company, named Gorkha after the historical little kingdom in Nepal, began to rock with the updraft, and it seemed that it would crash any minute. Not only was the seatbelt broken, but the seat itself was shaking and I had to hold on to the back of the seat with my hands. No, things like the seatbelt didn't even matter. If the plane crashed, it would be difficult just to salvage the dead bodies. It seemed that the plane was playing out a situation just prior to a crash. Anyway, in that urgent moment when my life was in peril, I suddenly recalled the apple in my bag that I took from the hotel cafeteria that morning, and so, looking out the window in the rocking airplane at the snow-covered mountains, thinking that I could easily die that moment, and chewing the apple as though in quiet meditation, I thought what comfort it brought to eat an apple for the last time in an airplane that could crash, and as I did my heart did in fact calm down and great joy came rushing in (and it was while I was quietly eating the apple on the dangerous airplane during the half-hour flight that I came up with a story about an apple with teeth marks on it on a bench in the kingdom of Budapest, which will develop into a story about dentures in the end, and which I may tell here).

I couldn't tell why the swallows were doing such a thing, but they looked as if they were deriving some kind of a pleasure from doing it. I suddenly recalled that when I was little, I saw the same thing, meaning swallows swooping down and brushing against the river and soaring, countless times at the river in the summer, and that I swam in the river, and at times jumped from the branches hanging over the river.

Anyway, I raptly watched the swallows that seemed rapt in doing what they were doing, closed the book I'd been reading, and very much enjoyed the stunt being performed before my eyes. I wished that the swallows that swooped down and brushed against the water and soared would keep on doing what they were doing, and the swallows kept on doing it as if it were nothing at all to grant such a wish, and kept on doing it even when, after a while, I thought it would be all right for them stop now, and kept on doing it, giving me no heed, when I shouted to them in a loud voice, in my heart, to stop it this instant, and kept on doing it when I said in a somewhat dejected voice that I wouldn't tolerate them if they didn't stop it this instant, now, so I said, in a faint voice, that they should keep on doing it if they had to, if they had no choice but to do it, if it was something that couldn't be helped.

The performance by the swallows went on for over an hour, and in the end, I whispered, What you're doing has nothing to do with me, but what's more, it has nothing to do with yourselves either, and only after a while did they fly off somewhere else as if nothing had happened in the meantime.

But even after the swallows stopped doing that strange thing and flew off somewhere else, I calmly made my swallows go on kicking the water and flying up for a long time in my heart, and I actually felt excited, as if something somewhere inside me were giving me a kick and calmly soaring, and therein lay my idea of a moment of fiction. Perhaps it was because I am infinitely drawn to things that are caught up in some kind of a blind passion, and feel driven to describe such things.

And the excitement continued until after I had a dream that night about a bird suddenly appearing out of a bowl of soup, lightly beating my face with its wing, and soaring into the air and flying out the open window, leaving a little fish, with only the bones remaining, floating in the soup bowl (I'll probably be talking about the somewhat strange dreams I've had as well).

It's difficult to trace the details of how I came to write this story, its origin, or source. The source of everything can be either nowhere or everywhere. Saying this, however, doesn't help at all in finding the source of something. And at times, revealing the source of something does not lead to an understanding of it. But what lies at the source of something? This question doesn't help, either, so let's narrow down the question and ask, what lies at the source of thought? What do you finally reach when you cast a thought back to another, like a fish that swims upstream, or like the act of going upstream to find the source of the river itself? But you can see, without thinking deeply about it, that empty thoughts lie at the source, just as nothing lies at the source of everything. And perhaps thought in itself is something whose source cannot be reached and the source of a thought that can be conceived is something that can't be reached even in thought. (Here I have no choice but to give up on thinking. I may also be making an attempt to circumvent the source as I write this, or I may be growing distant from the source but, at the same time, going toward it.) Perhaps you could say that there's no source to this story, or that there's a myriad of sources.

Thus I feel tempted once again to think, perhaps to my own convenience, that contrary to what I've said so far, this story began when I was sitting on a rock in a forest a while ago picturing a manuscript, like an unfinished posthumous work, that's on or near a hand of someone sleeping or lying as if dead, or lying dead, in the faint moonlight shining down on a forest of perpetual night in which eagle-owls are flying from tree to tree.

But this story may have begun in another moment, when I found myself walking, quietly listening to the sound of my own footsteps, on the stairs leading downward to a dark basement and upward to the roof where bright light was shining through, and through corridors with open or closed doors, while carrying something that looked like a birdcage—but no sound of birds came out from within—whose contents couldn't be discerned, or which didn't contain anything, or a lamp—but no light leaked out from within—in a building I somehow ended up entering in a strange city. Or it may have begun in the moment when I, in mist-shrouded Venice, thought of something as I pictured a child jumping on a trampoline somewhere in the city (I'll probably talk about that moment in this story). But it's probably useless to look for the source in this way.

With that, I'm not prepared to begin, but I will. But how, and with what, do I begin? It doesn't matter what I begin with, but I'd have to choose among countless stories, since I'll have to begin with one. (I have already begun, and have come a little ways from where I began, and what I'm writing is headed in an unknown direction, but it feels as if I haven't even begun, as if I'm hovering outside this story without even having entered it, and I could go on feeling, even as I go on writing this story, that I am just beginning, that I haven't even begun when the story is over, that I'm back to square one in the end, and in order to make that happen, I may have to wrap up with a story that makes you feel that it's going back to square one. Nevertheless, I feel that this story has begun to manifest some kind of an essence in some kind of a form.)

I should limit what I talk about to certain subjects, since I can't think about everything, and talk about everything I think about. I could begin with certain thoughts that have a strong or loose hold over me, and certain subjects made up of a series of these thoughts, things I've thought about for a long time and thought about linking together, death and travel and everyday life, for instance, and an overlapping mixture of these things, and see, with a bit of curiosity, how the subjects that I think could link together do link together in the story. In the process, I'll add thoughts to certain memories, bring memories into certain ideas, and link separate images into successive images (this story is also a story about the process of writing a story).

What if I began by talking about travel, which contains countless scenes from everyday life and is a metaphor for death? I could do that. But traveling isn't something I like all that much. I do think about traveling a lot, but I haven't actually done a lot of traveling, and although I don't dislike traveling I don't like it very much either. Perhaps I could rephrase this statement by saying that although I wouldn't go so far as to say that I detest traveling, I could venture to say that I don't like traveling that much (this story, in a way, is about rephrasing a sentence in different ways.)

What it is that I'll be writing seems to grow clearer as I recall, along with my memories about swallows, the travels I've done, and think about travel, which is considered an escape from mundane things and everyday life. This story could be a record of mundane things as well as a kind of a travelogue, a travelogue that contains casual yet cold ridicule on the many travelogues that praise and encourage traveling, and thus is for people who don't like to travel, and it could be a story that could give some kind of a hint, although it wouldn't serve as a good guide, on what to do when you don't know what to do when you're traveling, just as you didn't know what to do when you weren't traveling—if I were to write a real travel book, that's the kind of book I'd write.

And this could be a mixture of a journal and an autobiographical novel, something that's difficult to put a name to, or it could be something that isn't anything at all, or something that's not something that isn't anything at all.

But I think I should hold off talking about travel until later. Right now there are other thoughts invading my mind. Other thoughts are invading me, holding me captive.

What are the thoughts that are closest to me now, or, in other words, thoughts that are holding me captive, clinging to me and not letting go, by which I'm held captive? But couldn't I say that I'm not letting go of the thoughts by which I'm held captive, that I'm clinging to the thoughts, instead of saying that I'm held captive by the thoughts? Anyway, the thoughts are such that the more you try to break free from them, the more you become captive, but at the same time, they are such that the more you let go, the longer they linger (this story is also something that digs up and pulls out something dreadful that exists in thought itself, as an intrinsic part of thought).

Something is doing that to me this very moment, a sentence. My mind, again, is occupied with thoughts on the sentence, "Colorless green ideas sleep furiously." The sentence, presented by a language philosopher, is holding me captive like a charm, and I float around on it as if it's a raft floating on an open sea. The sentence, cited by the language philosopher as an example of a grammatically correct sentence, or in other words, a sentence that has a logical form but makes no semantic sense and thus has no intelligible meaning, and can be discussed at different levels, feels to me, at least, like something that navigates the sea of language with infinite freedom. What I thought of as I watched a dolphin-shaped tube floating down a river in a little town in France, too, was a play of ideas using words.

For the past several days I've been spending time reading mostly works by linguistically experimental poets, thus allowing passages from the American poet John Hollander's poem, "Coiled Alizarin*'" such as the following, dominate my everyday life.

> *Curiously deep, the slumber of crimson thoughts:*
> *While breathless, in stodgy viridian,***
> *Colorless green ideas sleep furiously.*

But wasn't it possible that the large dolphin-shaped tube I saw by a riverside one winter day, floating down the river, wasn't something that someone had thrown out? That perhaps the person sent something floating down the river every winter around that time, at that place, as if performing a sort of private ritual, and happened to set a dolphin tube afloat on the water that year? Wasn't it possible that he didn't wish for anything as he let go of something that floated down the river—I hope he didn't wish for anything—and merely wanted to see something float down before his eyes and fade away and disappear? And that no one knew he did such a thing every year, that it was his secret, his greatest secret?

---

*   A red pigment extracted from the root of madder, or produced by synthesizing anthracene —*Author's note*

**   Turquoise pigment, or the color thereof —*Author's note*

Yet as a result of his secret act, someone ends up thinking about plays of ideas as he walks side by side with a big dolphin-shaped tube that's floating down a winter river, wondering how it's come to float down like that.

Amusing ideas and games of ideas. Games using ideas, and languages, which are carriers of ideas. A story that's a puzzling game, a game that becomes puzzling. Games using words, just for fun, not just for fun, not necessarily for fun, for fun only, not just for fun only, simply for fun, in the spirit of fun, as if for fun, not possibly for fun, and in the end, for fun only. (Games using words are really the only games you can enjoy until you get tired of them, or enjoy forever without getting tired of them.)

Again, I feel that my craving for amusement is relentless, which isn't because my heart is heavy, both when I'm alone and when I'm with someone, or when I'm doing something or doing nothing, and seek to lighten my heavy heart. It would be more correct to say that it springs from the idea that life itself is a chaotic wandering state in which you roam around the edge of blindness, or make your way to the center of blindness, without any aim or will, and end up playing the writing game, having no other choice, and by so doing turn your life into fiction, fiction that resembles a riddle.

Perhaps the fact that the ideas that play around in my head often turn into something preposterous and bear and breed extravagant daydreams, or delusions almost, delusions that take up a great portion of my thoughts, when I think about it, could work to my advantage as I write about amusing ideas. For example, for someone who raises a lot of rabbits in his mind, rabbits could be something that gives him the hardest time. If he scoops out something sticky and slimy and transparent from the pond every morning, and imagines that it turns into several rabbits and gives them all the same name, Alice, and imagines that they take care of him and live only for a day like mayflies and hop around the pond, rabbits named Alice will be important creatures in his reality, and dominate him with real power, and he could say what a hard time he has because of the rabbit Alices that never leave his mind, and could be sad one day to find that all his Alices are dead. Although this is a metaphor—the rabbits are a metaphor for ideas or imaginations—the many ideas that come to my mind as I write this actually dominate me like the rabbits that belong to someone who raises the rabbits he scoops out of a pond.

Anecdotes in my memories and images in my imagination dance on a stage from which time, which flows in one direction, has made its exit. I wave at them, and further, I dance with them. The past is revived in the present, and I pass again through past moments. As I write this, I'll come face to face with returning scenes from the past and become a part of those scenes, and the scenes will overlap with my present, and I'll confuse the past, present, and future tenses.

Anyway, what I thought was a dolphin-shaped tube may have been a little plastic bag someone had thrown away, or perhaps I never saw such a thing as a plastic bag, or went out to the riverside and watched the river one winter day when I lived in a little town in France long ago. But I've already said something about a dolphin-shaped tube, and although it's an unreliable or nearly fabricated story, it becomes a part of this story, as words that are written down and printed out take on certain power and become a part of a certain story.

But it doesn't matter if what I think I saw by the river was a dolphin tube or a plastic bag, or if I didn't see anything at all. What matters more is the sentence, "Colorless green ideas sleep furiously," which I think came to my mind at the riverside. And recalling the sentence, I think again about writing something about the difficulty of existence, the difficulty of talking about the difficulty of existence, the double difficulty of it, which I think I thought about at the riverside as well.

But did I, at the riverside, begin, out of nothing, a vague groping in the dark that wasn't a new, careful search but a groping for a new failure that sought to end up as a failure, and think of a loosely structured story, that turns from a vague groping in the dark into a haze, and in the end comes to nothing, and think that such a story could be effective in writing about the double difficulty mentioned above?

And did I think that I could have something of an expectation in the fact that in the act of indulging yourself in a game of ideas, not knowing to the end what it is that you're talking about, and rendering it null, there's an innocent or a naive pleasure, like that of a game indulged in by a child at play, and think that there's something about a child playing alone that makes you think that in a way, a solitary game, with everything around you, and further, the world vanishing and leaving you alone, was the only real kind of game?

And did I think that I could obsess over what it was that I

sought to do because it was something I couldn't figure out, and something useless, and that I wanted to trust the feeling that things upon which such things could exert greater power were awaiting me, and that when you didn't know what it was that you wanted to write, you could do certain things you couldn't do when you wrote, fully aware of what it was?

My mind is all confused again. My thoughts, which raise their heads at once like Medusa raising her many heads at the same time, cannot be cut off or paralyzed, so I have no choice but to leave them as they are.

So I consider a story dealing with an attempt related to the combination of a word with another, and the joining of a sentence with another, as well as a story about the use of language, and a certain misuse of language, which, in a sense, is an undeniable use of language, and the confusion and limitations of language and thought. (I believe that among the dreams dreamt by language, there are sentences that are impossible in themselves, or ones that seek to become something of a chaos. And a writer must be someone who also dreams the somewhat strange but captivating dreams that language dreams.) I also think about the sentence, "Colorless green ideas sleep furiously," as well as the sentence, "Furiously sleep ideas green colorless," cited by a language philosopher along with the previous sentence as an example of a sentence that isn't even grammatically correct, and the sentence, "Colorless ideas sleep furiously green," which I created by changing the words around in that sentence.

And I feel tempted to devote myself to making unfamiliar or erroneous sentences, like someone who has suffered damage on the part of the brain in charge speech and who, in a sense, is able to express himself more freely due to a loss of normal faculty of speech. (In fact, I feel extremely tempted to make sentences with grammatical errors that are utterly incomprehensible, and think that one day, I could perhaps write a short story, one at least, made up of such sentences only.) It would be a sort of warming up of thoughts, as well as practice in making sentences, and such practice could be helpful in thinking more freely, and writing the kind of confusing story I seek to write. And such practice could consist of making phrases or sentences such as follows.

The softly hardened hand of something that threatens wet sense by holding it up against the smiling, bent fire of a red rose; or, The sleeping snail enveloped in the wind passing through the forest, a playground for cats, that looks like a bunch of umbrellas turned inside out, ravaged by cats in passing; or, The wet appearance of a raincoat that comes to mind when you tilt an arm horizontally puts a stop to the dance by twisting an arm somewhere within a sentence that's startled by something that's being watched by commas holding their breaths; or, No matter what you say to the stinkbug that lives in a pillow with me, the words, Be careful, eagle, won't get through, it's because martens that have lost their stickiness in the net I cast in the sea are pulling the strap that's retreating forward, or because it's been long since the ship that sailed off, with parrots on board, and doesn't return, sailed off, no, it's not because of that, it's not because of anything; or, the path taken by certain goldfish that do high jumps all day long should meet an animal that lives underground, that waves its hand play-fully, instead of being found in the mind of someone who marches in place,; or, what you can do for the sick bicycle lying in bed is to hit a mushroom, instead of a volleyball, with the palm of your hand, throwing it up into the sky, and going to the future in this sentence.

I actually suffered from a sort of aphasia, and thought in a way that was closer to writing than speaking, and as a result had difficulty speaking and had an easier time putting my thoughts into written words, so I wrote down in a notebook a countless number of such sentences that made no sense, whose list could go on and on, and the making of which brought me a kind of pure joy (I feel, in a sense, that this story is a list of sorts, which could go on endlessly, deleted, added to, and corrected).

In the notebook were pages packed with names and numbers of people I'd crossed out, wondering how these people could have such narrow views, and recalling their faces the last time I saw them, and hoping that I'd never see them again, and then, in a moment of weakness, restored even while scolding myself for being weak, and on the page on which I had most recently written something down was the sentence, The thousands of question marks that have sunk to the bottom of the pond cannot rise above the surface through their own desperate efforts, and must wait for a lying monkey to smile while looking into a mirror, and although I didn't know how I'd come to write such a sentence, I was sure that I wrote it one night while drunk.

Anyway, the symptom of speaking such sentences is closer to that of Wernicke's aphasia, the effect of which is to speak in a confusing language whose meaning cannot be conveyed, than that of Broca's aphasia, which poses a great impediment in speech, or the Williams syndrome, which causes difficulty finding the right words, so that you would perhaps say parrots while meaning sparrows, or cake while meaning cookie—I think about the difficulty experienced by someone suffering from the Williams syndrome, who says curtain, meaning gown, and screw, meaning spring, as well as the astonishment you'd feel watching him. I think putting yourself in the state of someone suffering from a syndrome from which you're not actually suffering and being in that state may, at times, open your eyes to things you didn't know about yourself.

But this story isn't moving forward, and I'm going back to square one, for my thoughts have turned back to the things that serve as guidelines in writing this story, to things whose help I feel I need. Am I taking a step back in order to take a step back, not to take a step forward?

I think about forms of stories. But again, I feel, as I always have, resistance against a well-structured, complete story. Stories with an impeccable structure stifle me. A story with a clear plot, which inevitably becomes something about following someone's whereabouts, has become something that's nearly impossible for me to write, just as Paul Valéry could never write a novel because he could not use a sentence such as, "The marquise went out at five o'clock." For some time now I have naturally harbored antipathy against stories with a narrative, and now it has become nearly impossible for me to read such stories, which seems to be a natural course of development.

I'd probably do better to let the words write themselves, as if I were writing down something dictated by someone unseen, and introduce chaos into the story, as well as giving it some kind of a system, thus exerting much effort in writing a story in which it is difficult to find traces of a plot, a story without traces of a plot, only traces of an effort to remove traces.

And I'm somewhat curious as to what kind of a distorted story will result overall when you devote yourself to the details with no thought to the overall structure. One of the reasons why I don't write stories with a clear structure or theme is because there's something about such stories, in and of themselves, that make me shudder with their boredom, and another, because just one look at our reality will show you how far removed such stories are from our reality—or my own life, at least—and how different the truth of our reality is from what's depicted in them.

What I can write is a story that's not quite a narrative, and is much too obscure and unstable. Not being obsessed with a completed story will create an opening into different territories in novels. A story with gaps and cracks and leaps and loopholes, a story that's incomplete somehow, may more faithfully reflect real life. What exerts the greatest influence on my life is things without substance, and I'm turning my life into something without substance, and as I regard the struggle against things without substance, or tangible substance, as the only genuine struggle—this problem of mine seems to be a fundamental problem of the world as well—I have no choice but to clumsily write something without substance.

Make it a story, if possible, that's not full of the power of narrative, a story seeking to break away from narratives whose naivety makes you smile, narratives that are dull because of their inherent tendency to seek power, and because their dull ideas are generally audacious, and their audacious aim to enlighten is inevitably dull. The persistent tendency in me to prevent the unfolding of a story, and the belief that there's no narrative to life, could perhaps make that possible. There are, of course, people who believe that there's a narrative to life, some of whom seek to turn their own lives into something with a narrative, through whatever means possible, and some of them do so with ambition, and some write narrative texts, and some reveal their ambition without hiding it, for it's difficult to hide such an ambition when you have it, but among such people, there are probably some who come to realize that in the end, their lives can't be a narrative, and that a narrative is not a principle that penetrates life, and turn their attention to something that's not narrative. What I want to write is something that depicts the fragmentary aspects of life, which are like a tangled skein, in a fragmentary manner, something that reflects my own life, which in itself is a great chaos, by creating and maintaining chaos, the greatest constituent of life.

Perhaps I seek to write something that's fit to be read on a rock in a forest you come to while on a daily walk, or in a café on a street where you're traveling. I would bring into my story fragmentary stories whose pages, turned by the wind, can be read at random, stories that allow you to close your eyes while reading and dwell for a moment on a scene that can be taken out from the book and savored, stories that are far from being narrative. Even when I talk about the anecdotes, they will be stories that are not quite narratives, stories that cannot be narratives. Perhaps even as I talk about the anecdotes, I could talk about my impressions on the anecdotes and the thoughts created by those impressions, preventing the anecdotes from developing into narratives.

What I seek to emphasize as I write this story, which perhaps says nothing, and in which something becomes nothing when the standards are changed, or whose meaning or importance changes (some of the stories I tell could end up being told somehow even though I had no intention of telling them, or tried not to tell them. And there will be almost no difference between some of them, even if there's a difference between those that are told and those that are not told), is not the story itself, but ways in which stories are told (the ways would include saying something that doesn't seem to make sense at one glance in a clever way so that it does make sense), and ideas that prevent something from degenerating into a story—ideas that prevent a story, even as it is told, from developing into a story in the end, or at least into a complete story—or, since many ideas come from things, something that is developing into ideas on things, or thoughts on thoughts I'm thinking, or on the pleasure or the difficulty of thinking, or thoughts on pleasure or difficulty itself.

And I'd have to subdue the various voices within myself that raise themselves or speak simultaneously—some of the voices seem to plead some kind of a difficulty, and some of them are on their way to understanding a cruel, merciless heart—or give weight to one of the voices. I'd have to close my ears to the end to the nastiest of them all, and press and suppress it, the voice that comes from the part deepest within me, the voice that denies everything, the voice that is used to silence or has learned to be silent.

Perhaps that is the result of a certain conflict between a figure

I have designated as the first person narrator of the story I'm writing and myself, for it could be difficult for a narrator, who feels uncomfortable that the author's voice slips in, and that his autonomy is violated, and the author, who sticks his head out while hiding behind the narrator, to speak in one voice. I already sense that the figure I have designated as the narrator would spoil the fun of the figure identified as the author and dash cold water on the thoughts that the author has, possibly leading the author to stand up to him even more for fun, and the person actually writing this story could find himself in an awkward position between the narrator and the author, and have a difficult time arbitrating between the two and side with one of them at times, but find himself in an ambiguous position at times (perhaps this story will be written by at least three people), and I'd have to write so that a calm tone and a cheerful tone cross and collide like dissonance, so that the unity of tone is broken, and tell the darkest story in the most cheerful way, or vice versa.

Anyway, there are other thoughts I'm obsessed with now, thoughts about death. Thoughts about death, of course, have always followed me around, and I'm as familiar with death as I am with the spots on my body I've had since I was born.

In light of the fact that although many things in life seem predetermined, nothing, in fact, is predetermined, and that you yourself can decide everything at every moment, and if you think carefully, very carefully on that fact, there come moments in which suicide, the best choice you can make, becomes very alluring, and such moments come to me far too often.

What I think about mostly, however, is death in general, not suicide through which I would murder myself, and not actual death, but something abstract, like the memory of a day when you shivered terribly in the cold, or a feeling you had upon seeing an abstract painting, or a sudden thought you have when looking at a dead fish still intact on your plate in a restaurant.

It's summer now, and in full bloom by my bedroom window are trumpet creepers, which are known to be toxic, or which I somehow came to believe are toxic, though I don't know whether or not it's true, and which I could touch by reaching out a hand, over the wall of my neighboring house, and looking at them, I think of death once again. For some time I had indulged in the idea that the toxin in the showy flower could make me die slowly, or at least go insane, and felt a strong desire to eat a trumpet creeper, and at one time had to realize that desire in another way, by coming up with the sentence, When a trumpet creeper dressed in the wrong clothes is going round and round many horses, you need to make an effort to row and go to the bottom of the lake.

Summer was always the most difficult season for me to endure; in any case, it was difficult for me to feel that way about any other season besides summer. It was difficult, at least, for me to do so as I did about summer. And that was because I thought summer was a difficult season for me, that it was inevitably a difficult season for me, but there really were aspects about summer that gave me a difficult time. For several years when summer came around, I felt that the summer would be difficult to endure, and each time, summer came to me as a season that would take me to a point of no return. Thus, summer seemed to be a season I had to stand up to, and I thought I could write something about an exhausting struggle and tragic loss of a summer, with the title, "The Record of a Summer's Struggle," or, "The Record of a Summer's Loss." And I considered using one of them as the title of what I'm writing, but concluded that they were more fitting as the titles of certain periods you went through.

Nevertheless, I managed, barely, to endure through several summers that came to me, and was faced with another summer. And yet, although I didn't know the exact cause—for I didn't try to find out the exact cause—my condition was steadily growing worse, and so for a long time I had a sort of a belief, the belief that I, or my condition, wouldn't improve, that it would never improve, that it could go terribly wrong at one point, and the belief seemed excessive in a way.

But when this summer came around, I passed out in my house, as if through a miracle that comes to someone who has unshaken faith and clings to it, as if through the realization of a long-held belief, and the incident was something that had been foreseen through dizziness that had been growing worse for a long time, and I'd prepared for it in my own way, that is, by not doing anything. My terrible negligence of everything made that possible for me.

The physical ailment that I'd imagined would come to me, however, was seizure or leg trouble or something of the sort. I'd also thought at one time that if one of my legs became impaired, I could procure a nice cane, and with three legs, now that one had been added, take more complicated, rhythmic steps, which wouldn't be possible with two legs. (I actually took a very careful look at an old woman with bad legs at the park one day, taking modest steps, relying on a cane, submitting to a certain rhythm, and afterwards when I saw normal people walking, they seemed somewhat stupid and awkward. And if I carried around a cane, I could raise it and politely scare off a dog on a walk with its master, delighted to see me and about to come running even though we didn't know each other, and prevent it from coming toward me, or use the cane to make the dog come closer as it changed its mind while coming toward me and refused to come any closer, feeling threatened by the cane I was holding or by me, holding the cane, or, before all this happened, I wouldn't have to chase away the tiresome dogs one by one, for the dogs could lose their nerve early on, seeing the cane, and not come close. And as occasion demanded, I could scare someone off, acting as if I would beat him if necessary, even if I didn't actually beat him with the cane, or I could, using the cane, pluck a ripe apple or a rose, hanging from a branch or a vine reaching outside the wall of someone's house, at a height I couldn't reach with my hand. I'm of the opinion that anyone passing by should be allowed to pluck an apple or a rose hanging from a branch or a vine reaching outside the wall of someone's house, but once, I was caught by the owner while plucking a rose, and was somewhat humiliated. The owner of the house was a philosopher, well known to the public, and he was furious at me, as if quite upset that one of his roses had been stolen. The aged philosopher seemed to be of the philosophy that nothing that belonged to him should be taken away from him by anyone. But it was my philosophy, if I had any philosophy at all, that something so small as taking an apple or a rose without the owner's permission should be allowed on this earth, still the only planet among the countless planets in the universe known to have life forms. A world in which you couldn't pilfer a luscious fruit or a rose while taking a walk on a bright afternoon or in the middle of the night would indeed be a world without hope. After that I saw the philosopher in front of his house severely scolding a dog, though I'm not sure if it was his dog or someone else's, or what it had done, and he was scolding it as menacingly as he did when I plucked one of his roses. In other words, I was scolded by him just as the hapless dog was scolded. Mercy was possibly the ultimate sentiment that a human could have toward other humans and living things, but it seemed that he had no mercy. He always seemed fraught with anger, and it was possible that he became angry even with his desk or dishes from time to time.)

Nevertheless, the culmination of the persisting poor condition of my body in the form of dizziness seemed to be something that suited me as the final outcome although I hadn't secretly antici- pated it, and it felt a little like a miracle when it actually happened because I'd been hoping in my heart that something would throw my life, which was much too tranquil in a way, and almost unre- alistic—I had an earnest desire to disturb a stable condition, even as I sought stability—into confusion, albeit slightly.

When I was severely dizzy, I felt as if I were suffering from seasickness on land, and I accepted dizziness as my natural state of being by thinking that I knew that I was on a rotating earth because of my dizziness, and that dizziness was something quite natural you could feel on the earth, in this dizzy world, and some- times, even when I kept still, I felt as if I were standing on a slab of ice floating down the river, or as if I were falling slowly, while at the same time soaring with an infinite lightness, into a seemingly bottomless space devoid of gravity, but also as if I were sinking, like some kind of a sediment, deep into the ocean where enormous pressure weighed down upon me, and at the same time, I felt as if my entire body were a building that was collapsing, unable to endure its own weight after many years.

But the dizziness I felt was something that could not be described properly through any color, shape, texture, figure of speech, or anything at all (one day, it seemed as if the floor of my room were slowly tilting this way and that—one of the symptoms of dizziness I felt could be described in this way—and it seemed that if there were balls on the floor, they would roll around here and there, but the problem seemed to lie in that I couldn't free myself of the thought that my dizziness wouldn't cease so long as it felt as if the nonexistent balls were rolling around on the floor and I failed to make the balls come to a stop), and I was frustrated, while at the same time fascinated, by the impossibility of describing the dizziness—I felt a bit of joy that I couldn't describe the dizziness, which was purely because I was thinking about how easily the modifier "indescribable" was accompanied by the word "joy"—and thought that the only adjective that could describe it, inadequate as it was, was "uncontrollable" (but is this an adjective?), and that the dizziness some people felt was something that separated them from others, and would be as distinct and diverse as their personalities or appearances.

The moment I lost consciousness, I felt as if I were clutching the hem of a woman's long skirt, that I was grasping it with more strength in my hand than was necessary, but I thought that in reality, the strength in my hand that was grasping it was leaving, and when I woke up after being unconscious for I don't know how long, I was, in fact, loosely clutching the hem of the curtain on my kitchen window, made of thick velvet.

But what I couldn't understand, above all, was how I'd woken up by the window, which was several steps away from the living room, when it seemed that I was in the living room when I collapsed. Perhaps I walked slowly toward the window the moment I collapsed, losing consciousness, or crawled quickly, when it wasn't necessary, like some animal that crawls quickly.

The sudden swooning brought me a peculiar sort of pleasure, but I couldn't tell if it was because I could think that I was clutching a woman's skirt hem, even as I lost consciousness and collapsed—I wasn't sure, however, if this very Kafkaesque experience was an experience of Kafka's, penned in one of his works, or my own—or if there was an inherent pleasure that could be found in the loss of consciousness, a pleasure that could be found if you sought to find it. The moment I lost consciousness, I actually thought that I was pulling and taking off a woman's skirt, a daring yet rude thing to do, but one that was delightful in a way, and also thought that I couldn't help laughing, though it wasn't something to laugh about, but I don't think I actually laughed.

The swooning also brought a peculiar sort of satisfaction, for there seemed to be an infinite space within the dizziness of swooning through which I could spread out infinitely, after being sucked up into the whirlpool of dizziness because of dizziness. And the incident gave me a sense of anticipation, a great sense of anticipation, for more to come in the future (anticipation is a very strange thing, making you anticipate such things, and making you, at times, anticipate your own fall and decline above all).

Having woken up by the window, I felt as if I could lose consciousness again at any moment, and everything seemed like a lie, and I thought somewhat clearly that everything seemed like a lie, in a way that was different from the way in which life itself seemed like a lie, but that there was nothing strange about it. In the end, I felt an acute pain in my knee joint, which had been bad for some time, and while trying to focus on it, wondered, This pain, where's its origin, and when was its origin? but it occurred to me that these expressions weren't correct, so I wondered again, What is the origin of this pain? and wondered if this expression was correct as I lost consciousness again, and this time I woke up in the bathroom. I couldn't remember how I'd made my way from the window to the bathroom and why there of all places either.

Sitting crumpled on the bathroom floor, and feeling great sorrow this time, I thought that I'd never be able to regain my consciousness if I lost it again and agonized over whether I should stay where I was, hoping to get better, or go to the emergency room, and if I were to go to the emergency room how I'd get there, and thought that I'd never gone to the emergency room in an ambulance and felt an urge to do so, but in the end, I called a taxi, and while being taken away in a taxi, I clenched my hand tightly, as if I holding onto a string of consciousness which I'd lose forever if I let go, and thought that it wouldn't matter that much even if I did lose consciousness, as if falling asleep, on my way to the hospital, and again thought, somewhat playfully, that if I swooned again, I should make sure to grab the hem of a woman's skirt.

I got to the emergency room and lay on a bed without being able to properly explain my symptoms to the doctor, and as he took certain measures, I wondered whether or not I should let go of the string of consciousness, and felt a strong desire to do so, even while fighting against it, and saw the curtains flapping in the open window, and remembered that it was while I was staying cooped up in a hotel in New York that I thought, looking at the curtains that were flapping in the same way, that I wouldn't go outside unless a gigantic sailboat, with a full load and the sails taut with wind, entered through the window, and the memory brought me a strange, almost unbearable, pleasure.

But death, which someone said wasn't a part of life since you can't experience it when you're alive, passed me by. Or should I say that I passed by death? But even after I recovered somewhat and left the hospital, I had to stay lying down most of the time. On some days I had difficulty just going from my bedroom to the bathroom, and barely managed to do so, holding onto the wall that led from my bedroom to the bathroom and feeling as if I were walking in a desert, utterly exhausted from dehydration and the blazing sun. But my disease, which caused dizziness, didn't develop in a certain direction as I'd expected, or in other words, it didn't just grow worse. In a way, it wasn't progressive, and even seemed to be progressing unfavorably. In a way, that was quite natural. Like all diseases, the disease I was suffering from went through a cycle of relapse, temporary improvement, and sudden relapse again.

But through the disease, I began to change in many, no, perhaps not so many, ways. More than anything, I had great difficulty reading, and had a very hard time understanding sentences. It took several times more effort than before for me to etch a sentence in my mind, and in fact, I had to think as if I were etching words onto a metal plate, using a chisel or hammering a cleat.

Anyway, something else that filled up my mind, which was full of thoughts on death, while I was in such poor condition, was thoughts on everyday life, which became routine for me after I passed out and could do nearly nothing because of my dizziness, which became part of my everyday life, which led me to think about everyday life, perhaps in a completely new way. I thought about the various aspects and dimensions of everyday life, and the everyday life of which I thought encompassed everyday moments or period of time in which I thought about things, including facts that bothered me on a daily basis, such as the fact that humans don't even know their origin, let alone anything else, or rather, that they've never even found a clue as to their origin, let alone their origin, and wondered if they would learn their origin someday, and looked at a sofa that needed to be replaced and had a hard time deciding on the shape and size of the sofa that would replace it, because although it could be easily replaced, depending on circumstances, the replacement would be not so easy when I considered that the new sofa would be with me for several years, and looked at a cat I knew, having seen it many times before, walking drenched in the rain on a heavily rainy day when I also took a walk, drenched in the rain even though I was carrying an

umbrella, and looked at the leaves of a tree gently folding themselves, probably to protect themselves in the heavy rain, and wondered if it was true that certain leaves did so to relieve the shock
from the streaks of rain, and thought that those two things were
the most memorable of the things that happened to me that day
or week, or month, and thought about the thoughts I had even
in my sleep, and was amused by the thought that Jains and Zoro-
astrians existed in the world, and decided that I should put off
doing the laundry for a few days, which I'd been putting off for
a long time, and had the banal thought that nothing really mat-
tered, and thought about how I'd give my goldfish a proper funeral
if it died, and drank some tomato juice, and wiping the red liquid
on my mouth, thought about the Battle of Stalingrad, perhaps the
most gruesome of all the battles fought in human history, in which
soldiers, having run out of vodka, drank antifreeze filtered through
the carbon filters on their gas masks and sang in chorus a song
that was at times called "Four Steps to Death," and thought about
Stalin, whom I'd caught a glimpse of in a black and white documentary film looking somewhat sulky, as if left out by the two
Western leaders next to him who had gathered at the Yalta Con-
ference to discuss issues related to the Second World War after it
came to an end and were smoking and laughing somewhat face-
tiously, and as if feeling uncomfortable at the facetiousness of the
two leaders (he looks as if he's trying somehow to show the two
Western leaders who are rubbing him the wrong way that he's
not happy), and wondered what he must've been like as a boy full
of dreams, and thought that perhaps at that moment, he felt deeply
offended by the two Western leaders and thought, As soon as

I return to Moscow, the hub of the world, I'm going to come up
with a way to teach these offensive people a lesson, and make sure
they understand that socialism is a far more superior system than
corrupt capitalism, and I thought that perhaps that was the
moment when he came up with the seed of an idea that subse-
quently led to the tragic Korean War, and thought that if nothing
in the world was permanent, the current capitalistic world, which
seemed as if it would last permanently, wouldn't last permanently,
either, and wondered what kind of a world would follow a capitalistic world, and wondered skeptically if any kind of an ideal
world could indeed be ideal, and thought about certain facts
regarding Hitler, who, along with Stalin, was one of the greatest
dictators in history, such as the fact that he had severe mysophobia
and took nine baths every day, and being fastidious about his
hygiene, he always took a shower if he sweated while presiding
over a meeting or giving a speech—being passionate and often
using large gestures, he sweated quite a bit, and it's assumed that
he took a lot of showers to rid himself of the sweaty odor—and
that he received nine injections a day of a hormone extracted from
bull testicles in order to show off his stamina and maintain a passionate state of mind—Why did it have to be nine baths, and nine
injections of a hormone extracted from bull testicles, a day? Could
such trivia serve as clues to understanding Hitler, who drove
countless people to pain?—and that he didn't like smoking or
drinking and issued a special order to all German officers to eat
chocolate instead of smoking (did he think that eating chocolate
would help them endure the hardships of war?), and didn't like
cats in particular, and grew nervous and looked afraid when he

happened to see a cat, and thought about all the dictators in the world, who in themselves seemed quite fascinating, and about something that could be observed in all dictators, and wondered what that was, and also thought about something that all dictators could have thought about as they fell asleep, such as what they would have for dinner the next night, and thought that they must've thought about how to eliminate those who were absolutely intolerable even by their standards, although they found almost everything intolerable, and thought that all these thoughts occurred to me while I was drinking tomato juice, and thought about how much I hated all sounds that came through a loudspeaker, and wondered why Germans had no knack for humor, and saw a spot on my bedroom wallpaper that looked like a little boat at first when the wallpaper got wet in the rain, and began to look more and more like a battleship, and wondered how the spot would change in shape, and thought about the things I could mock in my heart as much as I pleased, and thought about my native language that still seemed immature as a language, and thought about how indecisive I was, and how difficult it was for me to decide on something, and how often, as a result, I went without eating all day because I couldn't decide what to eat, and thought about how much I enjoyed doing things that were meaningless in themselves and in light of something else, and wondered if I'd ever done anything with all my heart and soul, and seeing my boy do something strange, recalled that I, too, did strange things as a boy, such as hide in a forest of owls where there was no else around, spending my time looking quietly at something or not looking at anything, and hoped that my child would do such strange things as well, and thought about people who spent their lives doing something I knew in advance that I'd never be able to lose myself in, and about their lives, and thought that remembering the past didn't bring it to the present, but was like crossing an invisible, labyrinthine bridge between a certain point in the past and the present, groping the handrail, and thought about how Kafka laughed repeatedly while reading his own work and wondered if I had ever laughed while reading my own work, and thought about the authors whose works made me laugh as I read them, and thought about how most of the authors I liked were already dead, and thought that when I read their works, I sometimes thought that I was talking to the ghosts who wrote those books, and thought about the works of authors and artists I used to like but now felt were quite banal, and could no longer read or look at, and thought about something that could be called the evolution of a human mind, and thought about the banality I saw in everything, which grew beyond control, which I couldn't do anything about, and wondered what kind of a work I could be captivated by in the future, and thought about certain facts, such as the fact that T.S. Eliot's first wife was in a mental hospital for nine years before she died, that James Joyce's daughter was in a mental hospital for forty-six years before she died, that Paul Verlaine once hurled his three month old son against the wall during a fight with his wife, and that he wrote long novels about wars but he himself handed out cigarettes and chocolate at a facility run by the Red Cross before getting injured by shell frag-ments, and thought about Hemingway, who served less than a week at the battlefront during the First World War, and about

Hokusai, the Japanese artist, who said at age seventy-three that when he was eighty his paintings would finally make sense, and when he was ninety they would truly be the works of a master, and thought about how Balzac felt his death approaching and said that only Bianchon, the doctor in *Father Goriot*, could save him, and thought about the surrealist poet and architect who attempted to create a surrealistic, ideal garden in the middle of a Mexican jungle in the past century, and thought that an ideal world could exist only in ideal thoughts, and thought, while listening to Eric Satie, about the fact that he lived in extreme poverty in the later part of his life, and wondered if his music conveyed the sentiments of a man facing extreme poverty, and thought about what Salvador Dali meant when he said that Jackson Pollock's style was like the indigestion that goes with fish soup, and thought, while reading the original English version of "Jabberwocky," the strange poem by Lewis Carroll that's almost impossible to translate, that it could perhaps be translated if long footnotes were added, and also thought about staying in the English seaside village where he is said to have written *Alice in Wonderland,* and thought about how Freud was a cocaine addict, and how Trakl, the poet, drank chloroform and spent time lying on a sofa, hallucinating, and thought about Trakl's younger sister, who, invited to someone's home for dinner, gave a cheerful musical performance, after which she went into the next room and killed herself with a gun, and wondered why I felt at home with bizarre things and felt at ease listening to music that could make you feel uncomfortable, such as Schonberg's "Pierrot Lunaire," and thought that there was considerable reason for it, and thought that I was eating too much fish, and wondered how many fish I must've eaten so far in my life, and thought that I asked this question almost invariably when I ate fish, and thought about how I had to make a living by translating foreign languages, and thought about the many dead authors I knew who translated foreign literature and then stopped thinking about them, and wondered what it was that made me reluctant to write something that could be called a love story or novel, and thought about the fact that I was always trying to imagine an unimaginable world, and thought about the frantic nature of certain feelings I had, and thought about feelings that didn't last long, and feelings that, once there, wouldn't leave easily, and thought about the fights I had with mosquitoes from time to time at home, fights that truly seemed like fights, and thought that since plants died most of the time from too much watering, one way of keeping a plant from dying, though not the most sure way, could be to find out how often a plant should be watered by bringing a plant home and not watering it until it was wilting almost to the point of death, thereby finding out how long it can survive without water, and thought about the time I went on watering a plant I had even though it was clearly dead already, unable to easily accept its death, and recalled something that I seemed to have heard from someone, that pouring fresh animal blood into a pot of red roses turns the roses blood red, and thought that I could grow red roses and pour chicken blood or pig blood into the pot, and thought about the way my attention went from one thing to another, and thought about things that were theoretically possible but realistically impossible or unrealizable in the near future, and thought that for some time now my life has been a long and difficult and tedious yet pleasant struggle against realism, and thought that my favorite part of speech may be adjectives, and thought again about the limitations of my native language, something I always thought about, and above all, thought about a technical way of making long sentences in my native language, which had no relative pronouns, which made making long sentences difficult, and thought about the pain in my knee joint which I felt more often and acutely, and thought, in regard to that pain, about the process in which something physical was perceived, and thought about devoting my entire life to doing something I couldn't finish even in a lifetime, for instance, writing down all the proper nouns—which, even among nouns, were the most perfect in themselves, but unlike other nouns which might no longer be used, whose object of designation was always in danger of disappearing—in all the languages of the world, dead or still in use, and adding explanation and footnotes on those words, and thought, while scratching my thigh that was itchy with a mosquito bite, that you could see the world in a different way if you knew all the proper nouns in the world, although this was impossible, and thought, while having intercourse and looking at the full moon which happened to come into view out the window, about the fact that amphibians liked to mate when there was a full moon, and thought that I thought with too much articulation even though I got tired of doing so at times, and wondered why I wasn't easily drawn to simple and ordinary things, and thought that some of the things I wrote were things I came up with at a cemetery where Christian missionaries of the past were buried after being persecuted and decapitated, and thought that it might make me feel good to go to an office I happened to see one day while walking on the street, an office that was supposed to be a place of research on the magic art of shortening distances and the art of flight, and listen distractedly to the nonsensical things that the people there talked about, and thought about the obvious fact that if I hadn't been born I wouldn't have existed in the first place, and to that end, and felt indifferent about it, and touching some kind of a lump somewhere on my body, which I happened to find although I didn't know when or how it had formed, wondered what shape it would take on in the days to come, and thought of the times, while seeing something develop in a strange way, I thought of a reason that didn't seem appropriate as a reason for something, and thought that there didn't necessarily have to be a reason, that it was better for there to be no such thing as a reason, or to not try to find a reason, but still tried to find a reason, and after seeing the horrors of a war that's still going on now, thought of the strange goats I saw on television one day, which passed out even at the slightest provocation, such as the sound of applause or the sight of an open umbrella, and smiled to myself, and wondered if the goats, which looked as if they found some kind of a pleasure in passing out, found real pleasure in passing out, and thought that it was after I'd seen the horrors of a war that I smiled, thinking about strange goats, and recalled the masturbating monkey I saw somewhere while traveling, and thought about the misfortune of polar bears that were losing their home because of melting glaciers, as well as their daily hardship, and thought, not seriously, about the issue of Germans and Jews, or not thought about it at all, and thought, above all, about my body, which wasn't healthy, contrary to what people thought, and recalling the fact that Novalis, the writer, was an expert on mining, and Keats, the poet, was a licensed surgeon, wondered if there wasn't something I could do professionally besides writing, and having been constipated for several days and sitting on the toilet and applying great force to a certain part of my body, thought about the expression "with all your might," or "with your heart and soul," and thought that everything that was before my eyes at that moment was staying where they were with all their might, or with their heart and soul, and thought about things that could be seen endlessly moving (seas and clouds, for example), and things that seemed stationary but were moving (clouds and deserts, for example), and things that moved without being seen (deserts and excrement in the body, for example), and wondered what kinds of things in today's world would be considered uncivilized and barbarous to mankind in the distant future, and thought about how much despair or joy Newton must have felt while teaching math at Trinity College at Cambridge when none of his students showed up for his lecture, which happened from time to time because he taught in such an abstract way, and despaired at the fact that what I wanted to write more than anything, perhaps, was something without a beginning or an end, but that it was impossible, and above all, thought, somewhat irritably, about how irritating it was to think repeatedly about certain human concerns regarding human suffering, which would never come to an end, and thought about the artist who, suffering from Alzheimer's, tried to put herbicide in coffee, thinking it was whiskey (should I stop here?—this is the narrator speaking. I could stop, but I could go on as much as I want, and I do want to go on—this is the author speaking, in a more playful way), and thought about the fact that I could think only in a way that was much too complicated, and wondered if I might go insane, if only for that reason, and wondered if being able to think in a way that was much too complicated was a talent, whether it would be better to discard it or nurture it, and wondered why I liked to say something nonsensical in a clever way so that it made sense, and thought about how the expression "retarded" is used to mean stupid, and thought about some figures of speech and about using figures of speech appropriately or inappropriately, and looking at a bruise on my body, wondered how I'd gotten it, and wondered why I sometimes had bruises on my body I didn't know about, and wondered why I felt affection for other animals, and thought that, among other reasons, it was because they couldn't speak, and thought that there was rapport that was possible only between those who couldn't communicate through words, and while reading a book on mathematics and trying to incompletely understand or completely misunderstand an equation that was beyond my understanding, wondered, as befits someone who doesn't know math very well, if the fact that Bertrand Russell, who was a mathematician, among other things, was one of the passengers who sat in the smoking section and survived the flight that crashed in Norway in 1948, while everyone who sat in the nonsmoking section died, could be a mathematical event, and thought about the breed of dog called Russell Terrier, developed by Reverend Jack Russell of England as a fox hunting dog, which was good at digging the ground and catching mice and liked to romp around, and thought about or tried not to think about a life of writing, in which writing, which was clearly not a healing process, but seemed, though it wasn't clear if it was, to be a process of maintaining a symptom or the aggravation of a symptom, and wondered why I used certain words or phrases repeatedly in my writing, and why I felt pleasure in doing so, but didn't know why exactly, and so felt that it had something to do with making something burst like a bubble, and felt that repeated use of words or phrases resulted in something like bubbles in writing, and wondered if the pleasure I felt in watching these bubbles weren't like the pleasure I felt in quietly watching countless bubbles form in water, and wondered what to think of myself, who some time previously had decided not to write anymore, and yet was still writing, and thought above all about everyday life which was almost always seriously and severely tedious, and thought about the fact that my biggest problem was that I couldn't really get excited about anything, and thought about my chronic problems that mostly arose from bad habits, and thought that music, which had no part in my everyday life, could stay out of my everyday life, and recalled how I thought that we were all going past ourselves toward ourselves, as I parted ways with a cow I encountered on the road one day and gave apricots to, and, above all, thought about myself, who wasn't eternal, who thought about things that weren't eternal, and thought about things that I could make my own by imagining them instead of experiencing them firsthand, making them mine even more completely by doing so, and thought about the things I did even without any enthusiasm, and thinking about the life I've lived so far, and changing the expression to the path I've walked so far, thought about how smooth or not smooth the path has been, and thinking about the things that made up my everyday life, thought about how they made up my everyday life, and above all, thinking that I was repeatedly using the expression above all in a nearly meaningless way in this story, thought that these thoughts I was having now could be included and further developed in what I was writing, and thought about endlessly going on with such sentences, and writing a novel by doing so, and above all, feeling tempted to make and commit intentional mistakes in my writing, and thought about whether or not it was possible to make intentional mistakes (are mistakes something that can't occur through intention, and can they be committed only unintentionally? Is an intentional mistake a contradiction that's logically invalid?), and thought about a contradictory story that's logically invalid, and thought that what's important is what kind of a story is placed in what kind of a context, and thought about the question of placing a story in a nonsensical context in my writing, and thought about confusing up my own memories and tangling up the stories, and thought that even if someone read what I wrote and found pleasure in it, the result was something I hadn't intended at all, and thought about thoughts that could be thought in different ways depending on how you thought about them could be thought to a greater extent the more you thought about them, or thought endlessly, and thought that you exist or don't exist to the extent that you think, and thought about things that make no difference at all whether or not you say they're such and such, and thought that there was nothing but language with which you could play around as you pleased, and in this way, I could make and add to an endless list of things I thought about.

Everyday life is often seen as something banal, but also found in everyday life, along with the banal, are the most astonishing, terrifying, and bizarre, and nothing that seems far from everyday life takes place apart from everyday life. And what's banal is not everyday life itself but certain things found in everyday life. In everyday life there are moments that captivate you, because the moment you step into life's most ambiguous, enigmatic territory called everyday life you feel a pleasant, unexpected surprise. And such surprises are everywhere, waiting for you at home, in an alley around your house, around the corner on a street, a forest path, or even in an unfamiliar place you travel.

Someone could, while taking a walk near his home, see a sign that says "National Boiler Association" on the first floor of a building in a residential area he doesn't normally visit and be touched by it in a strange way, although he would have ordinarily passed it by without second thought. He could also think that the place, which according to the sign, was headquarters to dealers who were probably responsible for household boilers nationwide, looked too small to be the office of National Boiler Association, but the place, home to an association of people whose job it was to make hot water flow from boilers in homes nationwide and let you take hot showers, and sleep in a warm room even in winter, could seem even more mysterious than a secret political or religious society, or he could look at the sign and think that the National Boiler Association could be a social gathering of people who did something that had nothing to do with boilers, or a ghost organization that was involved in something suspicious.

Or he could come across somewhere in the city he lived in an office called Teddy Bear Association, but seeing that it was locked, to his disappointment—the place could look shut down already, with only the sign remaining—he could stand before the office for a long time, and suddenly recall the touching documentary film by Andrzej Wajda, the Polish director, on teddy bears, and think that although he really hated being touched by touching things in general, he liked how the film touched him. And he could think that if he hadn't seen the film about teddy bears that had been with people or people who had been with teddy bears, which, if he remembered correctly, although he couldn't be sure because it had been long since he saw it, showed the process in which an artist in Canada established a teddy bear museum and collected teddy bears from around the world, and showed faded photographs with teddy bears standing side by side with people nearly everywhere in the world, in a living room, on a beach, on a battlefield, in a spaceship, sharing their joys and sorrows, and showed Hitler in the last scene, looking quite impressive, surrounded by teddy bears, he could have passed by the office called Teddy Bear Association with indifference.

He could also go on a walk around the house he lived in, and see a white mongrel with a tattooed unibrow standing in front of a shop and smile, thinking that the dog, which looked stupid to begin with, looked even stupider because of the tattoo, although there was no telling why its owner had given it the tattoo, and laugh for a change, looking at the dog, which looked like the most dejected dog in the world, thinking that the dog, of course, hadn't given itself the tattoo, so the owner must have given it the tattoo, perhaps while getting a tattoo himself so that he could always be sure that the dog was his, although there was no knowing what he was thinking. And having a sudden flash of thought at that moment, that, for instance, Baudelaire went around wearing lipstick, he could name the dog Baudelaire, and think that a tattooed eyebrow would have better suited Baudelaire the poet than Baudelaire the dog, and that if Baudelaire the poet had a tattooed eyebrow, he would have written a poem about it as well.

And he could take a walk on a hill somewhere, and find a swivel chair that someone had thrown away in the bushes for some reason, intact but for one missing wheel, and go there from time to time and sit on it, turning himself lightly, and think about the many things that had happened to him in his life, or think about his life in which nearly nothing, you could say, had happened, and pass many pleasant afternoon hours, and remember that once, while he was on an island in the Philippines and sitting in a metal chair on the beach—the chair looked as if it were in use by someone, not abandoned—he saw a fisherman setting out in the evening on his boat with a net, and saw the cross etched on his bare back, thanks to which he was able to wash away the memory of a bad dream he'd had the night before, in which his dead father appeared carrying in one hand his other hand, amputated from the wrist, like a fish, and saying that he had fished it out of some pond—as if he had caught a carp or something—made the strange demand that he decide which of the single hand he was holding in his hand he would have, at which moment he felt an urge to write something solely about a chair, and lie on the grass and feel the world unfolding beneath him, an enormous underground world in which his father, too, lay, and imagine being slowly sucked into the world.

And if there were some sunflowers on the hill that someone had planted, he could fall asleep for a little while under the sunflowers, having gone to see them on purpose in order to sleep under them when they were in blossom, and wake up and for a moment in a dazed state, and, not knowing where he was, recall how once he felt that my existence was unreal, so unreal that he felt as if his brain were in a drawer somewhere in his house, and the rest of his body in the wardrobe, or as if his entire body were hanging on the upper branches of a tall tree nearby, or he could see a yellow sunflower with a short stem right above his head and be overwhelmed with a certain kind of pure joy.

And days would continue, days on which he could see that the gloom that brought him pleasure at times, but not this time, was expanding its range within himself, and feel nearly overwhelmed because of the gloom, and feel so gloomy that he couldn't face myself, and couldn't look at his own face that looked so sullen that it embarrassed him, and thus could stand against the gloom as if making a stand against an oppressive and brutal system but to no avail, and so, instead of standing against the gloom, he could try harder to be gloomy, or think that he could meet someone and spend some time in a natural way in order to dispel the gloom, but then think that he couldn't stand to have my feelings of uneasiness beneath his façade of naturalness pass on in their entirety to the other person, and that he'd have a hard time putting up with the unpleasantness he inevitably felt when he was with people, and think that perhaps he had no friends at all but could be satisfied with the fact, and, one day, he could get up the courage to go out and go to a street crowed with people, and be startled by someone suddenly shouting in a loud voice behind him and flee from the spot, and with a Christian fundamentalist standing with a large cross saying naïve and nasty and foolish things that screech in his ears but don't touch his heart, vividly demonstrating how terrifying blind faith is, saying that you'll fall into hellfire if you don't receive Jesus, that you should repent before it's too late, he could feel awkward and uncomfortable even though the Christian wasn't yelling at him, and feel sufficiently rebuked even though he had no reason at all to be rebuked, and feel somewhat grateful to him, even, but because there was nothing he could do about it, he could punish him by glaring at him, and come home feeling repentant, at any rate, and deeply regret his first day out in a while and stay cooped up at home.

And he could see a strange scene on television in which goats on a farm somewhere in the U.S. pass out at the slightest provocation, for instance, the sound of clapping or the sight of an open umbrella, and think that he could perhaps see why they did so but couldn't in the end, and think of the animals he'd seen doing incredible things, thus recalling the time he went to a volcanic island, where he saw a roe deer lying face down near a little crater surrounded by a thick forest, which had collected water and turned into a swamp, and a crow sitting on its rump pecking and plucking its hair, and smile, thinking that the act looked quite erotic. And the crow was plucking the roe deer's hair to use it in building its nest—the roe deer's hair probably came in handy in building the crow's nest—and the roe deer stayed still for a moment, not wanting to budge at that moment, it seemed, even while having its hair plucked, but in the end it got to its feet, as if to say that although it was all right for the crow to take a few strands of its hair without giving anything in return, it couldn't let all its hair be plucked by the crow, and looking more dejected than offended, went off someplace else, after which he could recall how happy he'd felt to have had the good fortune to witness the little drama in the forest next to the crater, which perhaps took place between the roe deer and the crow on a daily basis.

And on occasion, he could think of animals that do astonishing things humans can't understand, of which he knew quite a few, such as a cow that chewed and swallowed chickens whole, a water buffalo whose hobby it was to blow gusts of air into plastic bags, a badger that was found lying unconscious in the middle of a road, dead drunk after eating cherries that were ripe to the point of fermentation, and a parrot with a wounded heart that stayed with its head stuck between watermelons in a fruit shop, and think that perhaps by doing such things, they were, with joy and fury and despair, expressing in a difficult way the difficulty, and the joy and fury and despair, of living their daily lives as animals.

Or he could recall how, when he came outside after having lunch in a restaurant on a tropical island he visited, a cheeky and pathetic looking male monkey, which was tied to a tree in a corner of the shabby garden, suddenly lifted its colorful skirt and shyly, but at the same time brazenly, exposed its erect red penis as if to flaunt it. Thus he could detect something nasty, cheap, sly, and mean, almost to the point of evil, in the monkey, and although he wasn't sure if such traits were something inherent in the monkey or gained through experience while living with people, and didn't know why it did what it did, though perhaps for sexual reasons, he could think that it didn't seem like sexual harassment that could take place between humans and animals, or think that the monkey was perhaps openly showing its pleasure, which it couldn't bear not to show, or again, openly showing its displeasure, and if so, the act could have been an expression of good or ill feeling toward female monkeys, but of contempt or hostility toward humans. Or he could wonder if the monkey had been trained by its master to startle, offend, or please a stranger by doing so, or to do so whether the person was a stranger or not—in that case, it was up to the person to be startled, offended, or pleased, and not something for the monkey to be concerned about—or if the monkey wanted to show off its penis to someone, thinking it had nothing but its penis to show off, and so it couldn't help but show off its penis, if nothing else, and he could think about the reason why the monkey had, as if it were something it did all the time, or at least without showing any signs of surprise, and without showing any signs of wanting to surprise the person, so nonchalantly taken out its penis, the size of which couldn't be determined as immoderately small or large, or moderately large or small, or just right in proportion to its small body.

And he could return from the trip, and think that the monkey left a deeper impression on him than anything else he'd experienced on the trip, and spend some time thinking about it. So the monkey I encountered looked at me with a quite desperate look on its face, as if what it had just shown me was nothing compared to what it could show me, as if it were going to show me something more amazing, as if to see if I was ready for it, and so I couldn't help but ask, What are you so desperate for? and watched what it did with my hands on my waist, because the monkey seemed too outrageous, and I thought of the word conduct, and thought for a moment about the conduct of the monkey that had made me think of the word, and yet felt great admiration for what it had done, giving no heed to humans, or looking down on humans, and felt delighted, and although I didn't know what it was about to do, I thought about what there was I could do to help, to give some small aid in what it was about to do, but the monkey did nothing more, just blinked as if to say that although it didn't know how I felt about what it did, it knew very well how it felt, and I didn't feel the slightest honor at the monkey's inclusion of me in its sexual conduct, and could not respond favorably to its effort to win my heart, for the effort was too explicit, without any subtlety, so I didn't show much of a reaction and the monkey looked as if it regretted having lifted its skirt and exposing its genitals, which was understandable because it hadn't gotten anything out of me, and its effort had produced no results, but the moment I was about to leave the spot, thinking there was nothing more the monkey would do that was worth watching, it took its penis in its paw and shook it, not pretending to masturbate but actually masturbating, and I watched as if in surprise or as if there were nothing surprising about it, not having known for sure if animals other than humans masturbated, and although I didn't know if perhaps the monkey's master, thinking he could do anything for his beloved monkey, thought about what he could do and came up with the idea of teaching the monkey how to masturbate, and taught it how to masturbate, or if monkeys masturbated on their own, and although I felt that the little monkey touching its little genitals seemed somewhat brazen yet boring, I realized once again that humans and animals and everything in the world coexisted in a strange way, and didn't hide my joy at the realization, but the monkey, for some reason, made a face and didn't hide its uneasiness, and when I tried to pull its skirt back down, it became extremely angry and ran wildly around the tree, and ended up being bound up tight by its leash, and I wanted to give the monkey a bit of a hard time, something it deserved, but I wasn't sure what to do, and at that moment the monkey's master appeared, looking angry even though he didn't know what had taken place, and he could sneak off, thinking that he usually chose to lose courage in the face of someone angry, and think that one time long ago, he had the thought that there was something inherently funny about sexual things.

And it was while he was having intercourse with a woman that he had the thought that things of a sexual nature could easily be associated with jokes, and he could think that sex, while it was the most serious act that all mating animals took part in, without which preservation of species wasn't possible, there was something ridiculous about the specifics of it, the act itself, and that laughter at times could be the most fatal blow to sex, and it became difficult to concentrate on sex when you burst out laughing, and sex was one of the most typical things that could seem ridiculous and preposterous while you're doing it, and although it was okay to smile quietly in your heart thinking that, you shouldn't laugh, and the moment you realized what a funny thing it was to engage seriously in sex, sex could come to a funny end, and I could also think that sex was one of the things in which the absurdity hidden in everything serious could easily be encountered, which wasn't surprising since everything serious contains something absurd.

And he could go back to thinking about the monkey he'd encountered, and although he wasn't greatly inspired by the monkey's incredible, and in some ways, inspiring act, he could accept the monkey's act as its idiosyncrasy and be inspired by another fact regarding monkeys. And it was about a monkey that killed a human being, how a monkey in a Southeast Asian country climbed a tall tree and threw a coconut at its master, hitting the target and killing him on the spot, and the master, who made the monkey pick coconuts when he was alive, exploited the monkey, making it work without a break, and beating it when it didn't do as told, and he could think that in a way what the monkey did could be seen as an animal uprising against one-sided human abuse, which could be considered something that should be included if a history of the relationship between animals and humans were to be rewritten, and although there were many incidents in which animals killed humans, they were caused accidentally by excited or angry animals, unlike what the monkey did, which involved premeditation, which could be seen from a new perspective, and perhaps animals kept what humans did to them in their collective memory and quietly prepared for revenge against humans, as suggested by the research finding of some zoologists who observed chimpanzees collecting stones in advance in order to throw them at visitors who came to the zoo, and think that it was strangely inspiring.

And (here I'm making a list of everyday things) someone could quite accidentally find a sign indicating that there's an artificial eye research center on the sixth floor of a high-rise building, and very excited, suppress the urge to go there right away, and think that it's not a place you could easily visit with both eyes intact and that he isn't qualified to go there yet, but may one day open the door to the research center and enter and wonder why he feels great interest in physical aids, such as artificial eyes, false teeth, and prosthetic legs, and try to find out the reason.

As a result, he could think that perhaps it was because when he was young, his beloved, deceased grandmother wore false teeth, and the teeth she took out and put in a glass of water at night seemed both frightening and wonderful to him, and because when he looked at his grandmother's teeth, he felt as if they were glaring at him, even though they weren't the eyes of an animal, and that the reason why the teeth seemed frightening was because they looked like part of a skeleton, but a more immediate reason was because a very old man, who wore false teeth and seemed crazy and was short, frightened him, as well as a speech-impaired man who was bound to be found in any town, and another disabled man. And he could recall memories of the man, who came running from somewhere with all his might, though he wasn't very fast, when children were having fun playing, and chased them away as if he were annoyed that they were having so much fun, as if to keep them from playing in such a way, or in other words, having fun—which was understandable, for the man, who could have been crazy and was old almost to the point of death, could have been annoyed with children having fun, which may have seemed unsightly to him, and didn't want to see them when he himself felt as if he were about to die, at the point of death —and when he did, he always had false teeth in his hand, and what in fact the children were afraid of wasn't the man, who was as small as they were, but the false teeth with several teeth missing—perhaps he knew that the false teeth in his hand would frighten the children—and the frantic feeling they could sense in the man who was running toward them. And he could recall how later, when the man could no longer be seen, and children no longer felt frightened by his him, seeing his false teeth, and people said he was dead, he wondered what happened, above all, to his false teeth.

And he could recall how once, he looked up false teeth in a book because he liked to leaf through medical literature to pass the time and it suddenly occurred to him that false teeth were one of the many marvelous human inventions, and was pleased to learn that from ancient times, people have used false teeth made from hippopotamus or sea elephant tusks, or teeth from dead people, but they rotted easily, so before the modern days, when ceramic false teeth were devised, most people had bad teeth, and thought that he wanted to write a story about false teeth, and actually wrote a short story about them as follows.

One very cold winter's day long ago, I was standing in the courtyard of a royal palace, from which I could see Budapest, Hungary at a glance. The palace, which could be seen at a glance from anywhere downtown, looked bleak, and it also looked bleak downtown, which could be seen at a glance from the palace. It was still early, and although I hadn't planned on it, I was the first to arrive at the palace. The museum that used to be a palace wasn't open yet, and I was able to go into the museum and get away from the cold after waiting for a long time—I mostly stood around the heaters, like someone who had come to get away from the cold, or looked halfheartedly at works that were on exhibit far away, which would have suited only the tastes of the royal family in the past and didn't inspire any feelings in me—but the interior of the royal palace and the things therein seemed only to be conspiring to make people feel as heavyhearted as possible.

After I warmed up I came out of the palace building as if to escape and took a walk in the courtyard, thinking about what I should do next and looking down at downtown Budapest, which looked gloomy even at a glance, and found something startling on a bench in a dark corner of the garden, which looked like false teeth and were, in fact, false teeth. I sat down cautiously at the other end of the bench on which sat the false teeth, for when I saw the false teeth that were sitting quietly and solemnly at one end of the bench, I felt as if there were an octopus or a sea elephant sitting on the bench where, ordinarily, there would be a lost mitten.

The false teeth, which belong in the mouth, but were now separated from the lips that gently covered them and the teeth that softly touched them, and whose upper and lower parts were precisely overlapped, the teeth facing me and tightly clamped, looked as if they were smiling mischievously, or were angry, or quite meek yet very arrogant, and, depending on how you looked at them, they could look as if they were making any kind of expression. I was extremely surprised to find out that false teeth, consisting of upper and lower teeth, could make such a variety of expressions, and I, too, bore my teeth and made various expressions at them for a little while. No, I didn't actually do it, only in my mind.

As I did, I looked at the false teeth that were before me and thought that the teeth, which made me think of a helmet, although they didn't look like a helmet, containing memories of battles and honorable wounds, and had nothing about them that was a direct reminder of a helmet—did a certain helmet I saw a little earlier in the museum bear a natural connection to the false teeth?— should be endowed with some kind of a glory, but I wasn't sure if I could endow it with a glory that was fitting. Looking at the false teeth that looked like some kind of an installation piece, I wondered how they had come to be at that place, and who had placed them there, and tried to find clues about their original owner, but the only thing I could come up with was that he must have had no choice but to wear false teeth because his natural teeth went bad, and I thought arbitrarily that it was because the false teeth, which used to be a part of someone's mouth, told me nothing more than that.

It was possible that the owner of the teeth, who was traveling, was very absentminded and forgot that he had placed them there and gotten on a train headed someplace else in Europe, but that didn't seem very likely. Or it was possible that the owner, who was from the area, or was a traveler from another continent and could be from anywhere in the world, had gotten a new set of false teeth, and while agonizing over what to do with the old, which had become worn, even shaky, during the long time they were with him, and which he could have grown quite fond of— it was possible that he wanted to bury them someplace, perhaps in a cemetery or in his garden at home, wishing to give them a proper funeral—he put them in a public place, anticipating that the people who found them would be surprised for a moment, then extremely delighted.

Sitting in the courtyard of a royal palace in Budapest, looking at false teeth that had found someone who needed them because he had no teeth, and were now possibly discarded by him, I considered placing something somewhere for other travelers, but it was so cold that I could come up with nothing other than the idea than that it might be nice to place a pineapple lengthwise on a seesaw in a playground, or a skate on a slide, or a cool artificial eye on a windowsill in a museum, or a living lobster in a sink in a public bathroom.

Once, I thought about things you could put in your house, things that could make you feel good in a strange way when you stared at them in a bored and dazed state, unable to sleep, such as monkey skulls and artificial eyes. Of those, artificial eyes could be great ornaments, and one day I was quite delighted to learn after reading a book on artificial eyes that in the past glass was used as material for artificial eyes, but now acrylic resin was used, and not only were there artificial eyes of various forms, much fancier than natural human eyes, but there were three-dimensional artificial eyes, vacuum artificial eyes, and even moving artificial eyes as well, and because the movements of artificial eyes weren't as versatile as normal eyes, someone wearing an artificial eye should make a habit of moving his head along with the eye when looking at people or objects.

Anyway, I sat side by side with the false teeth in the bone-freezing cold, thinking stupidly that I could think about something that could warm me up, but no thought could warm me up. Instead, my teeth began to clatter and shake—I was clenching my teeth and it wasn't easy to clench shaking, clattering teeth, but although the cold was making me miserable, the sound of clattering teeth, which made their way through the inside of my face to the ears, was pleasant—and while looking at the false teeth that were looking at me as if to say that they felt sorry for me, I pictured most people from the king down, before the invention of the modern false teeth, whose mouths looked disfigured with rotten or missing teeth before the invention of the modern false teeth—just as certain people in tropical regions all had red teeth because they always chewed on a certain fruit—talking to each other and laughing or getting angry, and forced a smile at the false teeth and thought about what to do with them. It didn't seem that I could leave them without making up my mind as to whether I should keep an eye on them, or leave them to their own.

In the meantime, snow began to fall again and thickened, and it was growing as dark as night even though it was morning, and even lightning struck in the distant sky. If not for the cold weather, the teeth and I might have sat side by side and chatted like people who had met on a walk, having a hard time thinking of right things to say. So as the snow that was piling up on my head and shoulders piled up on the false teeth, a conversation about how someone who had never stayed up a night on a bench in the courtyard of a royal palace in Budapest on a cold winter's day couldn't say anything about what it truly meant to gnash your teeth might have taken place between the teeth, which looked as if they had stayed up a long, cold night on the spot, and me.

But it was so cold that I could no longer sit on the bench with the false teeth, so I checked to see if anyone was watching and then put them stealthily in my pocket even though I could have been picking up something someone had discarded, after which I realized that stealing someone's false teeth was a very thrilling thing to do. And at the same time, it seemed as if I'd done a good deed, done the right thing, by taking the false teeth that looked as unfortunate as a kitten that had lost its mother and was begging you to take it with you.

In the end, the lovely false teeth that must have allowed their former owner to chew and swallow his food, smile with his gums showing in happy moments, bear his teeth at growling dogs, and perk up his ears to the sound of his false teeth clattering severely, shivering as severely as I was, on a very cold day, came to meet a new owner, and live a different life in a shoebox in my house, and became the best souvenir from my trips, and whenever I returned from a trip after that, the first thing I did was take it out and look at it.

But this unlikely story isn't true. It's true that I shivered in the cold in the courtyard of an old royal palace in Budapest, but what I found on the snow-covered bench when I came out into the courtyard after taking a look around the museum for a little while, having come to Hungary during the night although I'd originally intended to go to a city in Austria by getting on a passenger car of the wrong train—in Europe, there are many opportunities to get on a passenger car of the wrong train, and you can end up greeting morning in Italy when you had intended to go to Switzerland, but it's one of the charms of traveling by train in Europe—and discovering upon waking up in the morning that I had arrived in Budapest, was an apple someone had taken a bite out of, with clear teeth marks on it, and the story about the false teeth is something I made up. No, there was no such thing as an apple on the bench, only the trace of something like an apple in the form of a hollow semicircle in the snow. No, how about changing the story, by changing the previous statement, and experiencing a confusion of memories, or artificially creating a confusion of memories, or saying that I was confused, and saying that there was only snow on the bench, and no such thing as a hollow semicircle, or that I took out an apple from my bag and placed it on the snow-covered bench, or that actually, there wasn't even snow on the bench? What if by doing so, I made it impossible to tell how much of the story was true, thus turning the story about the false teeth into a fact that shows that what people commonly call a fact always contains something that's not a fact, that in fact, the boundary between fact and fiction is quite vague? So what if this whole story about false teeth is in fact a means of making up, in my own way, memories or impressions of my trip long ago to Budapest, to preserve them in myself in any way possible because I recalled the trip while eating an apple at home but everything about it had grown dim, as dim as if I had never taken the trip? (These words are proceeding dizzily among things happening between immovable facts and fiction that hovers around them, or between moving facts and fixed fiction, or among the things that I will make happen. By so doing, I'll be able to stand in the way of these words turning into a story, even if I can't keep them from doing so in the end, and I'll be able to keep them from turning into a narrative, at least.)

When I went to the royal palace in Budapest there was snow piled up on the bench there, and there may or may not have been an apple with someone's teeth marks on it on the bench, but through a story about false teeth I'm placing a teeth-marked apple on the bench there.

And in a shoebox in my house there's a set of false teeth, a plaster replica I bought in a souvenir shop on my way back from Budapest. Even now, I take out the replica from time to time and put it on a table by a windowsill and look at it. On this table, there's a flowerpot with a flower whose name I do not know, and a little statue of an ivory monkey, which is covering its eyes with its hands as if to say that there's nothing it could bear to see with its eyes open, which is what I like about the monkey statue.

Now, having written a story about false teeth, I take the replica in my hand and become lost in futuristic thought. All devices installed in human bodies, such as artificial eyes and prosthetic legs, elicit great admiration, probably because in them can be seen a model of the most primitive stage of the mechanical man, which could emerge sometime in the future—they'll be manufactured in factories instead of being born from the womb, but that, too, could be called a birth. This is the kind of thing I see in people who wear things like false teeth and artificial eyes and prosthetic legs, and I very easily think that they're people from the future.

In the meantime (from when to when does meantime here refer to? It's probably the period between when I began to write this, or when I became lost in thought after that, and this moment. And I could also say that it was when most of the trumpet creepers outside my window had fallen, and the grapes in the fridge had gotten all rotten and moldy, and I found that a lot of juice had come out of the plums I put in a glass jar with sugar, and I had finished translating part one of Virginia Woolf's *To the Lighthouse,* which ends with the Ramsays and the visitors to their summer home going to bed at the end of the day, and which I had been working on much longer than usual because I wasn't feeling well. Anyway, I feel as if during that time, I passed through a space like a river you have to swim across, and was carried in a rough current to a wrong place, completely different from where I'd intended to go at the beginning), I would often slip into a state in which I never went outside and let my thoughts float around, thinking about traveling, or perhaps about certain places. As the range of my movement decreased, and I could barely manage to go on with everyday life, let alone travel, I didn't become more and more desperate to travel.

I liked stories of adventurers, such as the story of Marco Polo, who wanted to reach the end of the world of his imagination, and Ibn Battutah, who traveled, endlessly deviating from his original itinerary, led by revelations and strange dreams—if his superhuman will was the light that led him, revelations and dreams seem like clouds that both blocked the light and let it shine through their cracks—but I didn't enjoy going on adventures. And I liked to have people tell me about the somewhat strange experiences they had while traveling, but didn't think about writing a travel sketch, for the experiences I had while traveling, which remained in my memory, were things that most people wouldn't find interesting.

For almost the first time since I've been writing, I think that I might talk about certain trips I took. But even if I do, what I write won't be an ordinary travel sketch. What I write will probably be as far from an ordinary travel sketch as possible, and not very helpful for many people, or not helpful at all for some people. That would be because essentially, there's nothing I seek to gain through traveling, and even if there were something, it would be nothing more than little passing impressions or some perceptual experience that would be difficult to explain.

And although traveling, in a way, is one of the only tolerable things that remain for me, there are many things that make it difficult for me to travel. First, I'm not very good at planning or pushing forward with something, but I can't very well stand traveling with someone, either.

In addition, my whims—alternating in my heart are the desire to do something, and the contrary desire to do nothing, which moves faster—and boredom, which follow me doggedly wherever I go, also make it difficult for me to travel, but the biggest reason is that when I consider traveling, the thought, What would I do if I did go somewhere? Nothing's going to change anyway, would present itself before anything else. In the end, the moment when it becomes possible for me to travel is when, very rarely, the thought, What would I do if I didn't go anywhere? barely manages to prevail over the thought, What would I do if I did go somewhere? But even when I end up traveling in this way, I often get caught up in a serious quandary as to why I'm traveling. Countless are the times when not long after I'd set out on a trip I witnessed and confirmed my reason for being there, which may not have existed in the first place, quickly vanishing, and I always regretted taking the trip, and at times gave up the trip midway through. And in part, my disposition itself, which makes it possible for me to feel utterly bored by anything and everything, which in a way is an inherent gift, makes it difficult for me to see and experience something new. What I found in traveling in the end was boredom, which wasn't different from the dreadful boredom found in everyday things, and boredom, indeed, was something that accompanied me wherever I was, and there was nowhere I could rid myself of it.

Thinking about travel and stories about travel while I was in a state that made it difficult for me to travel anymore, I thought about getting lost in my own story about traveling. Or in other words, making the story continue to deviate—the easiest thing would be to have other stories continue to make their way into the story to get a taste of the difficulty, trouble, and pleasure of getting lost in a story.

And yet there were moments in which I vaguely picture travel spots, which often included Tuvalu, the island nation that's slowly sinking and will soon be disappearing into the Pacific Ocean, and Madagascar, the island nation in the Indian Ocean. I know why I think of Tuvalu—it wouldn't be so bad to move to an island nation that will soon be disappearing into the ocean—but why does Madagascar come to my mind? The only thing I knew about Madagascar was that it broke away from a continent a long time ago and has been separated from the continent for a long time, hence its variety of unusual plants and animals, including all kinds of colorful and marvelous chameleons—which isn't surprising, considering that half of the chameleon species on earth live in Madagascar. Nevertheless, when someone calls me on the phone and asks how I'm doing, I say that I might be going to Madagascar—even though I know for sure that I won't—and tell them about the baobab trees there. But I could go to Madagascar, just to see the baobab trees which, according to legend, were placed upside down by a god who got caught in one of them and became infuriated.

A memory that has to do with Madagascar suddenly comes to my mind. It starts out with a French girl majoring in French literature, whom I came to know while staying in a small town in France, inviting me to her home in the country at the beginning of summer vacation (perhaps here, where I'm about to talk about something that has to do with Madagascar, I could attempt to get lost in a story by making a detour). Several days later I went to the small town where she lived and called her on the phone and she picked up, but she sounded quite cold, although I had no idea what had happened in the meantime, and told me to go back because she didn't want to see me, without telling me the reason, and I ended up being abandoned in a feeling of abandonment in the town I had arrived at after several hours of train ride. We sort of liked each other from the beginning, which could have been my imagination, but not quite, for if it wasn't true, she would've had no reason to invite me to her home.

There may have been a good reason for her to do so, or there may have been no such thing as a good reason—there may have been many reasons, or no reason at all—but I was a little angry at first, and after a little while, more puzzled than angry, and then more bewildered than puzzled, but I could accept what happened as something that could happen.

While on the train on my way to meet her, I pictured, with some excitement, a romance that could soon be taking place—it was summer, and thinking that there might be a little lake near her town and we might go swimming together (I pictured the beginning of our romance with us swimming in a lake), I thought that it wouldn't matter that I didn't bring my swimsuit, that maybe we could go skinny dipping—and the dismay I experienced upon arriving reminded me of the beginning of another somewhat strange—it becomes somewhat strange as I think about it—romance I experienced.

What you could call my first romantic relationship in college began while I was on my way home one night, taking a somewhat long way around to my house from the bus stop and going toward an alley. A girl was walking ahead of me, and we walked for a while, keeping a fixed distance between us, but sensing that someone was following her, she—I wasn't following her but felt as if I were, and the moment that I felt that she, too, could feel that way, I felt more certain of it—she quickened her pace and began to run in the end, sensing danger, and ran through the last alley into her house, and as I stood hesitantly in front of her gate, the gate suddenly flew open and a dog came running out. It wasn't a very large dog, but it came running out so fiercely that I stepped back and had to run in the end, but the dog, faster than I was, easily caught up to me and nipped at my trouser leg, making it impossible for me to go any further. Thus began our relationship, and we ended up seeing each other for some time because of that encounter, and she later told me that she'd felt, as I had, that someone was following her, and came out through the gate with her dog to give that someone a little scare, but the dog, which saw me at that moment, became agitated, and she let go of the leash—she said that she may have let go of the leash without really thinking about it, that she may have just wanted to do so—and that was why the dog came after me. For a long time after that, I would talk about the humiliation the dog inflicted upon me, and for a long time, she would talk about how ridiculous I looked in my humiliation. But I never told her about how once, when we went to a café together, and a dog there came running and went under the table we were sitting at and stayed there with its head stuck between my legs, I stayed still and let it smell the smell it wanted to smell.

Recalling that episode from long ago, I felt, despite the rejection, the kind of delight you feel when something ridiculous happens to you, so I didn't go back right away. Curiously, I wanted to further explore the town of the French girl who had made something absurd happen to me. The small town was a typical small French town, and it took less than ten minutes to walk from one end of the town to the other on its main road. I went around every nook and cranny of the town as if everything piqued my curiosity, even though there was nothing to see there.

That night, after roaming around the small town, I stayed at a little hotel there, and while reading *Molloy,* one of Beckett's Trilogy, which I bought and was reading at her recommendation, I thought about the Irish author who died not long after he said, while spending his last hours in a hotel in Paris, that he would die if somebody didn't change the horrible wallpaper.

I also thought about something I read in another author's auto-biography, something his aunt said before she passed away, her last words being, "That's interesting. Now I understand. Everything is water." She, who was a doctor herself, went to a dinner party where she met Chekhov, a young doctor who later became an author, and she offended him somehow while having a conversation with him on medicine, and made him express his anger toward her in a letter he later wrote.

That night, in a hotel in a small town in France, I thought for a long time about how you could spend your dying moments. Since dying moments could be important to anyone, or could be considered important, I could think about them for a very long time, and then maybe get a small live octopus and spend my dying moments with it, thinking that the only thing left for me to spend my dying moments with was an octopus, and feeling a certain gratitude toward it for that, and time it well and die at the same time with the octopus, which can't live long out of water, or die thinking that I'm following the octopus which died before I did. Or I could go buy an octopus a little earlier, and spend my remaining hours, the rest of my life, with it, and die with the realization that there's no difference whatsoever between the death of the octopus and my own. And I could realize anew, or not anew at all, the fact that death is what eliminates the difference between every living thing, which isn't anything new, and that everything becomes one before death and extinction, as I share my fate with the octopus. And looking at the octopus, I could mutter, That really strange looking green cat looks like a pineapple somehow, and think, But even as a pineapple, it looks somewhat strange.

And looking at the octopus, and continuing to think about the octopus, and recalling the black pebbles I think I saw once, glistening with water on a pebbled beach, under a blazing summer sun, and the octopus wriggling among the pebbles, I could think about how the octopus wriggled, how many black pebbles there were on the beach, and how black they glistened, and how, looking at them, I felt a certain joy at the fact that they would glisten with water for a long time to come, perhaps even after mankind disappeared, and how absorbed in the joy I was, and wonder which beach it was where I thought I saw the countless pebbles glistening with water, or if the wet pebbles glistened incredibly under the bright moonlight because it was night, not midday, or if it was pitch dark night and I saw the pebbles glisten momentarily because of the light from a lighthouse, or if I heard, between the sound of foam constantly breaking, the comforting sound that pebbles make as they roll around, crashing somewhat uncomfortably into each other, the sound that makes you feel that your heart is being carelessly caressed, but not uncomfortably, and above all, if I had ever been to such a beach, and think that what I was trying to recall was not an octopus wriggling among pebbles, but black pebbles, glistening with water and reflecting some sort of a light, or the countless beams of light reflected by them, and wonder why I had recalled, of the many things I'd experienced or thought of in my life, black pebbles glistening with water, while at the same time breathing my last breath, feeling pleased that I had recalled them.

And in the hotel room where I was staying, there was a flower-pot with daffodils in it, and it didn't seem like a bad idea to leave my will to the daffodils. So I said in the direction of the daffodils, as if leaving some kind of a will, The treadmill left behind by a squirrel that left on a search for a new path must meet more than three unfortunate ends, regardless of who takes it; in any case, the daffodils that were either in full blossom or were budding, had a shape that seemed fit to talk to.

And it occurred to me that in the act of talking to daffodils there was an element of an aside in a play, which is uttered with the assumption that someone is listening, different from a mono-logue, which is uttered when no one is listening, even though the daffodils couldn't talk back, and I may have felt this way because I felt that the flowers, at least, listened to every word of what someone said.

In any case, daffodils were certainly better than shoes to talk to, feeling as if you were talking to each other, and if there was some-thing else that was decent to talk to, it would be something like a fedora. I thought that I could blurt something out to daffodils before I died, and that the act would bring some kind of a pleasure.

I also thought about writers who, like Oscar Wilde, couldn't stand their own countries, and tried to abandon them, such as Beckett and Thomas Bernhard, and I thought about the country in which I was born and raised and still living, and thought that the biggest thing I tried to accomplish in the country was to leave it permanently, even though there wasn't really another place I wanted to settle in.

I fell asleep thinking such thoughts, and when I woke up the next morning I was able to think almost nothing at all about the girl I never ended up meeting. But while having breakfast at the restaurant on the third floor of the hotel, resenting the girl, who could have rejected me for a reason she couldn't tell me, or explain herself—this because the waitress who brought me my food, who was around the same age as the girl, made me think of her—I saw, through a window whose curtains were drawn, two workmen who were replacing the round red roof tiles on the roof of a house across a little alley that was about the same in height as where I was sitting, and I was pleased beyond words. They worked very slowly, and I ate very slowly as if to keep some kind of a pace with them. And I was able to eat slowly because I was lost in thought, about an anecdote which I wasn't sure was true or not, about Salvador Dali, who supposedly painted the droopy clock in the painting "The Persistence of Memory" not long after watching, as if in a trance, the camembert cheese that was melting on a dinner table. On the table before me was, in fact, a plate holding two pieces of cheese, which I placed deliberately where the sun was shining to make them melt slowly, and as I watched them melting and changing in shape, not as if I were in a trance but as if I couldn't take my eyes off them, and tried to think of something other than what Dali must have been thinking of as he watched the camembert cheese melt, or in other words, what he must have been thinking of as he tried to see the camembert cheese before his eyes as something else, or, in other words, tried to see it as something that couldn't be thought of as something else, and again, in other words, of something other than a droopy clock, but nothing else came to my mind other than a droopy clock.

But at that moment, I saw a crow that flew over to the roof where the workmen were, and through a process of association, I thought of van Gogh, who killed himself with a gun he claimed to have borrowed to shoot the crows that annoyed him, and suddenly wondered if he didn't shoot himself, mistaking himself for a crow, and where exactly he killed himself with a gun. He could have done it while painting in his studio, while crows cawed loudly outside, or while standing absently before an easel with a brush in his hand, not being able to even think about painting because of the crows, but I fancied that he did it in a wheat or corn field while a flock of crows watched him. As he died, he could have thought, You win, but this isn't your or anyone else's victory, and if you must determine whose victory it is, it's the victory of the corn field, where countless corn kernels are ripening. And as he slowly bled to death, the crows could have fled for a moment, startled by the gunfire, and then returned and spent the day eating grains, after which other painters could have come to the spot where van Gogh died, and painted the wheat or corn field where crows were flying around, cawing loudly, or sitting.

And I also thought about a gifted American cartoonist who mostly did sexually abnormal drawings, who said in a documentary film about himself that he always felt suicidal whether he was drawing or not, and whose life itself was more fascinating than the cartoons he drew, and his morbid younger brother who ended up killing himself, and about another younger brother of his who also drew cartoons when he was a child but became a drug addict, who in my opinion was even more gifted than his older brother who had become a famous cartoonist.

All through the meal, and after the meal, I was still hungry, not only because I ate little, but also because I ate very slowly, thinking about people who had committed suicide, which also pleased me. The breakfast, which I actually started eating somewhat late in the morning, came to an end at last at lunchtime. And picking up a yellow flower that was on the plate I had polished off, and picking out the petals and eating them one by one, I thought of crocuses, thinking that it looked like a crocus but was certainly not a crocus, and recalled the fact that crocuses that bloom in spring are called crocuses and ones that bloom in fall are called saffrons, and thought about how certain facts that were insignificant in reality pleased people at certain moments, and I was mostly pleased by such things.

And the fact that I was in a situation that was still obscure but no longer seemed so unpleasant, in which I had come to a strange little town to see a girl I didn't know very well, whom I knew nearly nothing about and who knew nearly nothing about me, thinking of possibilities of one kind or another regarding her, then was turned away, made me feel so content and pleased that I had to smile, for it let me devour the yellow flower that made me think of crocuses, and think arbitrarily, after finishing the last of my coffee, and looking at the dregs, that my luck had run out.

And after a short while, when the workmen took a break even though they hadn't done that much work, and lay sideways on the roof enjoying the warm rays of the sun, I too buried myself deep in my seat, and bathed in the peace of the little town that could be seen out the window. I heard the quiet murmur of people talking near the kitchen, but there was no one else at the restaurant. The town made you feel as if everything were passing slowly.

It looked as if the workmen had fallen asleep in the sun, and a very light breeze stirred up their hair and shirts and pants, taking them into pleasant dreams, and the breeze, which had come in through the open windows of the restaurant, was taking me into such a state as well. On the rooftop there was a weathercock in the shape of a rooster, which kept stirring very slightly and then stopping, for no other reason than that there was a very light, irregular breeze, and it seemed as if the rooster, too, were sleeping and dreaming, squirming lightly. The rooster, with a red comb on its head, was moving very minutely, and seemed to be quietly enjoying everything about the moment in its own way.

Anyway, there was a framed painting hanging by a window in the restaurant, which depicted a scene that was almost exactly the same as the scene out the window, seen from where I was. When I moved a little to the side, the painting looked the same as the scene, as if I were where the artist was when he was painting it. But there were no workmen in the painting, and there was a crow sitting on the top of the rooster-shaped weathercock, and when I moved my gaze from the painting to the scene outside, there was a crow sitting on the weathercock. The crow was at an angle slightly different from that of the crow in the painting, but it still looked like the crow in the painting. The scene seemed just perfect for looking at while passing time in leisure after breakfast.

I suddenly recalled that Napoleon kept "Mona Lisa" in his bedroom in the Tuileries Palace for some time. Perhaps he could feel, while looking at "Mona Lisa" before he fell asleep, that he really was an emperor who enjoyed all the privileges in the world, and felt that the greatest of all his privileges was having "Mona Lisa" in his bedroom and looking at it before falling asleep. Perhaps there was no painting like "Mona Lisa" to hang in someone's bedroom. And perhaps Hitler tried to lay his hands on "The Art of Painting," an enigmatic painting by Vermeer, for the same reason. Looking from the scene out the window to the painting depicting the scene, I felt that, in that moment at least, I was enjoying some kind of a privilege.

In that small town, there was a feeling of coziness found in all places where everything happens so slowly that time, too, seemed to pass slowly, and the feeling allowed me to stay lost in leisurely thoughts that rambled on because they were leisurely. I recalled my long-held belief that the roof, like the living room, should become a part of everyday life, and that people should spend more time on the roof, and also thought that the roof, indeed, was the most peaceful place in the house, that most quarrels take place in the living room or the kitchen, that people don't go up to the roof to quarrel, and that the roof is a good place to calm yourself down when you're angry. But soon it occurred to me that if the roof became a part of everyday life, a lot of quarrels could take place on the roof, which then could become even more dangerous than the inside of the house.

I came out of the hotel and went to the station that was at the hub of the town, and even when I was on my way to the station, I was thinking that I could go to the Lascaux Cave, which I knew was not too far from the station, and see the paintings there and think for a little while about how short the history of the present civilization was, and how it hasn't been that long since humans came out of caves, or go a little further to the island of Mallorca, where Chopin wrote the "Raindrop Prelude," and spend time in a room there listening to the sound of rain falling, or by a window where the sun shone through, feeling, to my heart's content, an anxiety different from what Chopin felt, preferably of an unknown nature, or go to Turin, the city that Nietzsche, who planned from very young to write a little book of his own, and who in a way carried out the plan, said was the city he loved the most. Turin was also the city where Giorgio de Chirico, who saw countless riddles in the shadow of one human being, read Nietzsche, found "a strange, profound, mysterious, and infinitely lonely poem" in Nietzsche, painted "Melancholy in Turin" and "Spring in Turin," and said that the city was the source of a series of his paintings, found melancholy. Perhaps in Turin, you could feel, as Chirico said, statues "come to life, talk, and even begin to walk, and come down from the pedestal and disappear." Turin, where you could pass by countless statues depicting humans in squares and streets, as if passing by passersby, seemed to me like a city of statues, a city where the silence of statues ruled over noise. It seemed that in such a city, I might be able to dispel the gloom that always accompanied me, or at least feel differently about it. But it was certain that Turin was no longer the Turin that Nietzsche loved.

But for some reason, perhaps for no reason at all, I began to walk along the street opposite from the one I'd come from. Perhaps it was because of a vague thought that came to me while I was looking at a gently winding railroad track several hundred kilometers outside the train station, at the railroad track beyond the curve, which disappeared, drawing a curve, or came from beyond the curve, or stayed where it was as a curve, and bending the curving railroad in my mind into an angle that would make train service impossible, or while I was watching a station employee waving a flag, as a train left after coming into the station and stopping for a moment. Or maybe it was because at that moment, I thought, Here's a man who came to see a woman he knew nearly nothing about, who knew nearly nothing about him, and he's in a dilemma because the woman, who invited him, rejected him for some reason, and he's somewhat curious as to what would happen to him if he stayed in her town for a little longer, so let's give him a little time and see what happens to him, making him walk into a story, one way of which would be to give him a little push and let him walk as his footsteps lead him, and with that thought, I began to walk blindly, and felt that I was walking into a story with him, entering naturally into a story. And I might have thought that when you don't know what to do, especially when you don't know what to do, you can do something that makes you feel even more as if you were doing something that didn't make sense, that you should do such things, and that I could do any number of such things, thereby trying to convince myself with a thought that wasn't very convincing even to myself.

I cut across the town and walked along a little country road that suddenly began where the town came to an end, and when I thought that it was like Molloy's town, it really seemed to be Molloy's town, although I wasn't sure what resemblance there was between the town and the idea I had in mind of Molloy's town, and then there were hills and forests there, and the landscape and terrain were such that the place may well have been where Moran, a character in *Molloy,* wandered around with his son, so it was fit to be called Molloy's town, and it occurred to me that it was because of *Molloy* that we became friends soon after we met, and again, I wanted to meet the girl who had stood me up but resisted the desire, and thought somewhat absurdly, but quite benevolently for her, that perhaps what she'd wanted to do for me was to let me roam aimlessly in Molloy's territory, thinking about him. And I thought of a vague story titled, "Roaming in Molloy's Town," and thought that I was already in the story, and, thinking about getting lost in your own story, kept on walking.

Looking at a white goat standing on a rock on a low hill, I walked around the hill to where the field began, and saw something blocking the path. It wasn't the goat I'd just seen. So it wasn't that the goat had come down in the meantime and was blocking my path. What was blocking my path was a cow.

Because the path was so narrow that someone had to step aside, we stood, hoping that the other would step aside, but the cow stood in a respectable and dignified manner, with no signs of being flustered. The cow had very large breasts with many nipples under the belly. Strangely, I felt a little intimidated before the cow, and thought that if I had a tail, I may well have lowered my tail completely. And I suddenly recalled the fact that T.S. Eliot was afraid of cows, and somehow I understood him completely, and wondered if one day, perhaps in his childhood, he had an experience involving a cow, which remained in his subconscious mind, and came to fear cows since then, or if he came to fear cows for no reason after seeing a cow one day, or after thinking a certain thought about cows, or if he decided to fear cows so as to think that there was nothing as frightening as cows in the world, causing a fear of cows to take root in his heart and body, as compassion or love for, or fear of, someone takes root and sprouts in the heart, but I had no way of finding out the exact reason. Perhaps Ibsen, too, came to have a fear of very small dogs for such reasons. But it didn't seem like such a bad thing for there to be something in the world you were particularly afraid of, whether cows or dogs, or a coat hanging on a hanger in a closet or a ball of yarn with a long strand of yarn unraveled on the floor, or the red comb of a rooster or the eyes of a dead fish.

And again, through a strange chain reaction of thoughts, and being aware that the chain reaction was working in a strange way, I had the somewhat ridiculous thought that the misfortune of cows began when humans began to fill their hungry bellies with cow meat and bones, and as if that weren't enough, to squeeze out every last drop of milk from their large breasts. And as I thought about it a little more, I became curious as to what cows and sheep and goats and camels and horses and such thought of humans squeezing out every last drop of their milk, but in any case, they didn't seem to have any great complaints. No, it seemed that they did have great complaints, but were hiding the fact and letting their anxiety grow. Whenever I saw them quietly ruminating, it seemed to me that they were gnashing their teeth. Even though I had walked only a little ways from the hill where the goat was to the field where the cow was, I felt as if I had been wandering around somewhere for a long time, which pleased me even more.

Because there was plenty of time to think about who was blocking whose path—the cow seemed to be dawdling in its own way, as if it didn't have any pressing matters to attend to— I concluded that I was blocking the cow's path—the path, in fact, wasn't so narrow, so we could easily pass through without either of us stepping aside, and I thought we were blocking each other's path, even though it was more likely that I was blocking the cow so that it couldn't pass—but still, regardless of that, I was conflicted for a brief moment as to if the cow, which was bigger than me, should step aside, or if I, who was smaller but older, should, but I didn't think of it in terms of us being human and not human. But in the end, I, a civilized man, gave way, and broke off a piece of a baguette, a staple in the French diet, that I happened to have on me at that moment, and proffered it to the cow, which sniffed at it and declined, not because it couldn't tell if it was edible or not, but, as it seemed to be saying when it looked at me, because it couldn't trust me. So this time, I gave the cow the apricots which I also happened to have on me. And the cow ate them, and blinked its eyes a few times in my direction as if in gratitude, but again, it looked dignified, without making the kind of a face that some animals do, asking for more, when you give them something to eat. I felt pleased to have seen the cow eat the apricots with relish, and I felt grateful for the girl who stood me up, and for the fact that I was stood up, and felt almost happy because of it. After a little while, the cow, which would soon be forgetting its encounter with a stranger, went on its way, looking carefree, and I, too, went my way, feeling carefree. As I walked away from the cow, which I thought must be feeling good because of its encounter with me, I felt that my steps had become lighter, and regardless of that, looking back at the cow, I thought that we were all just going past ourselves to arrive at ourselves.

Anyway, at that moment, something that often frightens me

happened and I was about to get diarrhea, and I was put in a sit-uation that required that I run into the forest nearby, but I didn't like to run so I walked into the forest, barely managing to keep the diarrhea from spilling out, and as I relieved myself (so far in my life, I've never run in fright, or away from a great danger, but countless are the times when I've had to run to a nearby bath-room or woods because of diarrhea), I thought that there was no song that I'd prepared for singing birds, when there were no singing birds, or at least, no sound of singing birds, and I let the birds that must be singing a song somewhere do the singing, and I became lost in my thoughts. Anyway, as I was relieving myself, I saw mushrooms, which I couldn't tell were edible or not, but seemed edible because they weren't colorful, growing here and there around me, and picked a mushroom near me while having diarrhea, but I couldn't tell whether it was okay to eat it or not, or whether it was good for diarrhea or not.

I suddenly remembered how someone who often experienced crisis as I did because of diarrhea told me that he always carried around a roll of toilet paper in his bag, and had relieved him-self in the woods a few times, on which occasions he broke off a branch that his hand could reach and put the toilet paper on it, and whenever he did, he felt very pleased because he felt as if he were relieving himself in his own toilet in the woods, and I thought that I could do the same in the future. Perhaps I could show, by hanging a roll of toilet paper on a branch in the forest, that someone was relieving himself in the bush below. Or a roll of toilet paper could come in handy when you go into a forest where you might get lost and want to make your way back out, and it would also be helpful in a strange city where narrow alleys are intricately intertwined like a maze. In that case, you could mark your path by tearing off the toilet paper piece by piece and throwing it on the ground. This method could be very helpful in London, England. According to an investigative report, London is the easiest place in the world to get lost in. In London, the chances of getting lost are twice as high as those in Bangkok or Beijing, which is twice as large in area as London, with one out of every ten people getting lost in London, because one out of every three Londoners give you wrong direction on purpose. In light of this report, it would probably be better not to ask for directions in London even when you're lost. (By letting the story deviate like this, I could remain in a state like that of being lost in a story. I can't prevent the stories that branch out of a story and deviate from doing so.) In addition, Germans are the best at finding their way, and they say that one third of all Germans have never been lost. This goes to show that Germans, who prepare for things thoroughly in advance, are an amazing people who suffer from an obsessive compulsive disorder. And they say that one out of every ten Russians ask for directions not because they're lost, but in order to seduce the opposite sex.

Let's come back out of the deviating path in the story and get back into the forest in the story. And through a strange process of association—even in that moment, my diarrhea was in progress, and I thought this diarrhea was a long and grueling diarrhea—I suddenly recalled the fact that when Beethoven lived in an apartment in Vienna, Austria, he kept a chamber pot under his piano, and, once, a visitor found that it wasn't empty, and I thought, to my advantage, that it was an appropriate thought to have while having diarrhea. Perhaps Beethoven was afraid that his inspiration would vanish if he went to the bathroom while composing, and kept the chamber pot there so that his inspiration wouldn't be cut off, even if his excrement was cut off in the chamber pot on which his buttocks were perched.

After relieving myself and spending some pleasant time on my own, I stayed with the mushroom in my hand, not knowing what to do with it, and then I remembered how once, I went into a forest with someone and saw mushrooms in great abundance, just as I did now. We picked a few edible looking mushrooms, but at that moment, an old woman appeared from somewhere and glared at us as if we were trespassing on her territory, but didn't say anything. We weren't sure if it was her mushroom farm, but we told her nevertheless that we were very sorry, but she remained silent, even when we asked her if we could keep the mushrooms we'd picked, and if we could eat them. She looked at us for a moment without saying anything, as if she weren't interested in people at all, and looked deeper into the forest, in a way in which most people would have difficulty doing, as if she had forgotten how to interact with people, as if she had never learned how to interact with people in the first place, or as if she were making irrelevant remarks to evade the question. Her mind was occupied by something deep in the forest, whatever it was, and not by the mushrooms around her, and that's where her attention was.

She went off somewhere else without telling us if she wanted us, who stole mushrooms on her mushroom farm, to become sick or die, or if she, too, had come to someone else's mushroom

farm in secret to steal mushrooms, or if she had simply been passing through at that moment, and in the end, we threw away the
mushrooms which we couldn't tell were edible or not, and I had
no choice but to do the same with the mushroom I'd picked in
the forest in the town I thought of as Molloy's.

I went a little deeper into the forest and climbed a little high,
clearing a path through the trees, and soon I reached a spot that
could be called the peak. But the peak wasn't very high, and it
seemed that it was more like a little hill than a mountain.

I sat under a tree, leaning back against it, and looked at the
scene spread out before me. It seemed to me that the scene was
somewhat too open, as everything in sight is, but I didn't care. A
typical French country scene lay before me, and I stared at it as if
there were something infinitely captivating about it and as if I were
trying to be completely captivated by it, or as if I were endlessly
resisting it so as not to be captivated by it, or as if I were trying
to be at least somewhat captivated by it even though there was
nothing captivating about it, as if it were all the same, or not very
different, as if I were in a trance, and, at the same time, indifferent.

And with conscious effort, I used my eyes to gently return
the still scene, which had spread out wider before my eyes in
the meantime, no, the scene that I thought had become wider
even though it was the same, and had not become wider in the
meantime, to its original size, and looked it up and down. A cloud
that looked like a flock of sheep was drifting in the sky—it didn't
look that way on the whole, but I tore off a part of it in order to
see it that way—and I thought that there's nothing like a cloud in
the realm of nature that could transform itself so freely, and that

that's why I never tired of looking at clouds, and saw several birds flitting among the branches in front of me, and heard the sound of birds singing, which must have gone on before I got there and then ceased for a moment.

I felt that I'd stepped into a lyrical world—I thought that perhaps it was because I had come, anticipating a rendezvous with a girl, which didn't happen, but it seemed that it wasn't necessarily so—but in that scene of nature, which was far from a scene of ruin, I saw some sort of ruins, and then it seemed that I was in a lyrical world that couldn't really be called lyrical, a lyrical world bereft of lyric, a lyrical world that had come to ruins, or a world that was the most lyrical because it was in ruins—is a lyrical world lyrical because there's a harbinger that everything in it, nature and civilization all, will one day vanish and come to an end, that in the end, only ruins will remain, and only an enormous shadow of the ruins will linger?—or in some sort of ruins, in another strange lyrical world, and I was fettered to that world. And I thought that it could be because nature, which was perhaps purely blind, was spread out so languorously before my eyes. As I had such thoughts, it seemed that the scene of nature served as some kind of a background music for my thoughts, and the music sounded squeaky and disordered, like a wrong tune, which kept me from thinking properly. The music was like the sound of orchestra members tuning their instruments without the conductor present.

But the sound I wanted to hear at that moment, the sound the wind makes as it passes through a forest, caught by trees and then escaping, or the sound trees make, holding the wind for a moment and then freeing it, could not be heard. And yet the branches in the upper part of the forest were stirring slightly. I suddenly remembered how I used to go to the forest near my house when I was a boy, and climb up to the top of a tree where you couldn't climb any higher and look at the forest where there was nothing to see besides other trees, and it seemed like a very strange experience. (My childhood before a certain period of time seemed time out of mind, like a previous existence, and it seemed that in my childhood, at least, there had been moments in which I was happy for no reason, but the fact didn't comfort me or anything, and in the first place, I wasn't sure if it was true or not.) The branches near the top to which I had climbed were shaking, and I had to hold them tight so as not to fall. But being at the top of a tree as if keeping watch, though there was nothing there that had to be kept under watch, excited me in a strange way. There were owls living in the forest, and sometimes I saw, from the top of a tree, an owl sitting at the top of another tree. Was the reason why I climbed to the top of a tree because I liked the idea that it wouldn't occur to people, and perhaps to owls, as well, that there could be a child on the top of a tree, where things like owls should be? Or was it because I seriously entertained, as children do, the fantastic idea that if I were to be born again, I wanted to be born as something with wings, not as a human who had to live with his feet on the ground, and to do so, I had to become friends with owls that lived in the sky? In any case, looking at owls from the top of a tree in a forest where owls lived, I imagined that we were staring at each other without moving, and felt safe, and protected although I didn't know from and by what, and whenever the persistent boredom and anxiety and loneliness of childhood visited me, I hid myself in the air.

(It's different every time, of course, but as I write this, my swimming in a river where swallows swooped down and soared up, brushing against the water, and jumping from a branch hanging over a river, and being at the top of a tree in a forest where owls lived as if I weren't there seem like certain clues or signs necessary in looking into and understanding my childhood, but they also seem like vignettes that don't require interpretation, and were sufficient as they were. Still, the origin of some of my thoughts, perhaps, and of the ways in which I feel about some things, or at least some of them, could be traced back to my act of hiding in a forest of owls, quietly staring at something or not staring at anything. But how insufficient and ambiguous is it to trace the origin of something in this way? Anyway, when I was a boy, I used to feel an urge to go down into the ground, as well as to go up to the territory of owls, and when I actually saw a pit dug by an animal, I would imagine going down into it and disappearing. Was this, too, something that provided a clue as to what I have become since then? Was I already very tired then of living on earth? Or did I want to go hide somewhere, as if I predicted the days to come? No, it was a very natural thing for a child, a very normal way for a child to create his own space and stay there.)

Thinking about my childhood, I rolled up my trouser leg to show myself a very old scar on my knee, which I got by falling down from the owl tree when I was a boy, even as I thought that it wasn't necessary to roll up my trouser leg like that, and thought somewhat absently about how far I had come from those days, and recalled some childhood memories that don't easily leave once they're recalled, and was sending them away with as much difficulty as possible, when a gentle breeze began to blow again, and a great distance away I saw something that looked like a flock of sheep moving very slowly, and the flock of sheep, which looked as if it were moving even more slowly because it was far away, was adding, perhaps unnecessarily, a new unity to the composition of nature that was already perfect in itself, and it seemed that the unity wouldn't break even if a movement of something else were added to the scene, with a flock of birds appearing or something, so I posed the question, Is a perfect composition of nature something that can't ever be broken by nature itself? but failed to obtain an answer, and so I thought that bagpipe music would be in harmony with the place, and that the place might have been the stage of the Hundred Years War, which continued on tediously between France and England long ago, and wondered if the soldiers played bagpipes even during the war, and if the enemies really fled in fright at the somewhat sad sound of bagpipes, even though bagpipes were originally played by the Scottish to frighten their enemies on battlefield. Bagpipes, whose inherent sound was plaintive, were often played at funerals for some reason, and I thought, Sometimes the sound is so plaintive that it sounds miserable.

And I thought that in the very forest where I was lying, feeling, even while lying down, the gentle breeze which came from the sea, with the Atlantic Ocean being somewhere to the west from where I was, though I didn't know how far away it was, soldiers slept during the Hundred Years War, and that some soldiers might have thought of another war that was fought there, and some of them might have thought of a story that was passed down from the time when Roman soldiers were in rule there. And I thought about how tedious it must have been to be at war for a hundred years, and had the somewhat absurd thought that the people at the time continued on with the war for a hundred years so as not to return to life before the war because it had been so boring, or that the people of England and France, who had opened their eyes every morning for generations, failed to find anything else worth doing as they began the day. Or, I thought, perhaps they continued tediously on with the war for a hundred years because they wanted to see the end of a war, like the end of a story, but the war didn't unfold as they expected and did not end easily, like a story that doesn't easily end, and I thought that I may not be able to end this story easily either.

Perhaps the people went about their everyday lives even during the war that lasted a hundred years. They must have been faced with the everyday routine of fighting, and they must have begun the day, after digesting their breakfast, with a weapon in hand— for it must have been difficult to fight without even digesting what you ate, and if you did, you would've had to fight, clutching your side in pain. And they must have fought for a short stretch at a time, not long, since they wore heavy armor, which must have made it difficult to even just remain standing while wearing them, and fought with heavy weapons in hand, such as swords and spears and shields, and sat or lain down and taken a nap in the shade of a tree after fighting for a little while, or sang to ease their fatigue and the longing for a loved one with whom they had parted. For there must have been nothing like a song to ease their fatigue and longing. In the meantime, a flock of sheep must have watched from afar, with extreme interest, the people fighting to take possession of the scene of which they, the sheep, were a part, and then grown indifferent to the fight among the people, for sheep don't stay interested in such things for long, and returned to grazing. And after repeating this several times, they must have become indifferent to the fight among the people and come to consider the war, which humans were waging without any regard to them, part of their everyday life. And in the meantime the field, which had been noisy with the sound of swords and spears clanging against each other, must have fallen silent as the soldiers, failing to resist drowsiness—for you can't fight while trying to resist drowsiness—fell asleep. There's probably nothing like a war, which makes its brutality so easily pervade everyday life, and becomes a part of ordinary life through repetition, that shows that it, too, can become a real part of everyday life, even though it's considered the furthest thing from everyday life.

I began to fall asleep, thinking that there was something in the pastoral scene that had once been a ferocious battlefield, that kept me, who had come from a distant foreign land and was lying without stirring in a forest in the French countryside, whose exact location I didn't even know, as if to hide from the world, from getting out of that state, and I thought that it would be all right if I fell asleep and never woke up. I also thought that it's harder to refuse small invitations to death, which come to you like quiet passion at such peaceful moments, than to overcome moments of unspeakable pain.

And I also thought, as I always end up doing when I fall asleep in a forest like that, that there could be snakes there and I could get bitten by a snake, but a snake wouldn't bite someone who was asleep, and wondered why I always thought about snakes when I fell asleep in a forest, but more than that, I thought that if I fell asleep, I could have a dream about the Hundred Years War in the middle of the battlefield where the war was fought. And I fell asleep, fancying that the clouds in the sky, which looked like a flock of sheep, were heading a flock of sheep on the field over which they cast a shadow, and feeling as if a long snake were gently climbing over my body, and thinking, What is that thing hanging from the tree, if not a leopard? though it was hardly likely that a leopard would be on a tree in a forest in a French countryside, feeling as if I were being buried snugly in the sand blown by the wind on a desert toward evening.

But when I woke up from a dream about chasing someone while being chased by someone else, a situation which, in dreams, makes everything seem drawn out and urgent at the same time, which ended with me entering a forest, and which I don't remember in specific detail—I did remember, though, seeing crows floating on a pond and thinking how strange it was—it was peaceful all around, as if the war really had ended long ago, or as if a war had never taken place there. But I suddenly recalled, while still half asleep, that I once dreamt about a forest with a bed and a table with coffee cups on it, as if my house had been relocated. In the dream, in which all objects had, to a large or small extent, lost their original shape and size, I spooned up a little cloud that was hovering low above my head and tasted it, but there was no taste to it. But when I put the cloud in a cup of coffee, the coffee tasted good as if it had cream in it, and the cloud went very well with the coffee.

I thought that it would be nice if there were pots of plants and a mirror in the forest now. If there was a mirror, I could lean it against a tree and see my foot, for instance, in the mirror reflecting trees. And if I tilted the mirror at a certain angle, I'd be able to see my foot along with a cloud in the sky. I thought of several more scenes that would look well in a mirror in a forest, which included me sitting in a crimson velvet chair with an earwig or a green frog, as if we were indispensable to each other. The reason why I pictured something like that might have something to do with my recalling that at a certain point in history, people began to view the world through windows, and that at a certain point in the history of art, people began to paint by holding up an object to the mirror and reproducing the image reflected in the mirror. Objects, and sceneries, do not lose their essence by being in a frame, but are endowed with a new essence, and become clearly different from before.

I looked at the scene again and it was beautiful, and there was something about it that appealed to the heart, although I wasn't sure exactly what it was. And when I pushed aside a branch of a bush that was slightly blocking my view, so as to get a better look at the stage of the Hundred Years War, I saw a fortress-like structure in ruins on a hill, which convinced me that a war had indeed taken place there long ago. The landscape that lay before me did, in fact, look like something that two countries would wage war over. (I also fancy that England and France went to war because the English couldn't bear to think that the French ate on a daily basis delectable wine and cheese, which they themselves couldn't eat, and wanted to keep the French from doing so, if not for anything else.) There must have been another reason, of course, for the war, one that was less romantic or lyrical, but I thought that waging a war so as not to let the opponent take possession of such a landscape, so as to take possession of it yourself, was quite reasonable as a reason for waging a war. And the region was famous as a grape and truffle producing district.

At any rate, people started many wars for ridiculous reasons, and did many ridiculous things even during wars. People of a certain period, thinking it would be advantageous to make spears as long as possible, did make spears as long as possible, and ended up being unable to even pick them up—they probably couldn't fight with them, for they couldn't even pick them up—and during the First World War, Italians, flaunting their remarkable fashion sense, made red uniforms that became easy targets for the enemy, reducing the chances of survival for their own youth. During a war, it's possible to see an antiaircraft gun in someone's garden, through laundry flapping in the wind, and in fact, it was possible to see such scenes at the time of the Pearl Harbor attack by the Japanese. Perhaps war is a stage that lets people do the most ridiculous things in the easiest way.

As I looked at the landscape before my eyes, picturing scenes from the past of people fighting, the herd of animals in the distance drew nearer. But I still couldn't tell what the animals were exactly. I was pleased to think how I had been led to think about the Hundred Years War, and to watch a passing flock of animals with interest, on this short trip I took to see a girl I didn't even know very well, who had rejected me.

In the meantime, things that were clear or unclear continued to appear and disappear, or stay, in clear or unclear forms, and I watched them without losing sight of them, or watched them, losing sight of them. And smelling pine leaves, I rejoiced a little, as if it brought me ineffable joy to smell, in a forest in a French countryside, the smell I'd smelled in a forest a long time ago in my childhood.

And a wisp of wind blew for a moment, and then it stopped. The wind seemed to blow, but then it didn't. And when I took a deep breath and breathed out long and slow through my mouth, the wind didn't blow as if my breath had stirred it up or anything. Nevertheless, the moment I thought that there was nothing I could do about this wind it began to blow, as if it had read my thought or was supporting it. Whenever the wind blew, I thought I had something to do with the wind blowing stronger, exhaling and adding breath to the wind.

And when the wind grew weaker, I exhaled more softly, and ,repeating the process, I recalled that I liked to treat objects as ideas, and ideas as objects, and thought that the wind seemed like some kind of an idea at that moment. Some ideas are sticky like ice cream melting in a child's hand, and are fluid, being soft like a jellyfish, but other ideas are solid like a hammer and can be used to drive in a nail, and yet other ideas are fixed, like a nail that's been driven in, and then there are things, such as certain birds that fly in a formation toward the equator or a polar region, that are ideas in themselves. (Endowing an idea with the shape and characteristics of an object, and coloring an object with an idea, is probably a task belonging to poetry, not fiction. I might be trying to make this become more like poetry than fiction.)

Thinking, This wind, at least, has a wavering belief, and is faithful to that belief which is bound to waver, I enjoyed the strange game with the wind, and soon got tired of it and forgot about the wind.

But looking at the grass, wilting in the midday heat and gently swaying in the wind, I recalled some thoughts about my existence that were deeply rooted in me, which were difficult to shake off, and it occurred to me that by thinking that the grass was wilting, I was inflicting injustice on the grass, and viewing it in an unjust light, so I withdrew my gaze, and the thought, and was about to root out the thoughts that were deeply rooted in me, which were difficult to shake off, but then stopped and let them take root even more deeply in me. And among those thoughts, the one that became the most deeply rooted was the thought that I was barely managing to stand, as if floating, on some kind of a foothold I couldn't quite or ever touch, since it never existed in the first place, that there were no grounds for my existence anywhere, which had more than enough grounds in me, but was groundless in itself if you thought you had found the grounds for it. The idea that everything in existence existed by accident, that inevitability was only a part of a tremendous accident, was something I could never shake off, and made my life so difficult, and yet so easy.

As I looked at nature spread out before my eyes, it looked as if it were weary, or bored, of being nature, of having no choice but to be nature. By and large, nature made me feel at ease, but at that moment, it looked much too steeped in self-satisfaction, and I felt somewhat uneasy. And the question I'd long had on my mind of why nature always looked natural rose to my mind again. If nature held a power that made everything that was placed in it an inevitable part of itself, what kind of a power was it? And other questions naturally surfaced among my thoughts that seemed as if they would come to a stop, again and again, but didn't. Were unnatural things something that only humans could create? Was nature, which seemed indifferent, obsessed with balance? Did nature not commit errors? Or was it free from errors? And was it because nature couldn't be accused of errors, regardless of whether or not it was free from errors? Was nature free of responsibility, and could it not be held responsible for something? Was nature free of responsibility for everything, including itself? But could you say that something was free from errors because it couldn't be accused of errors? Or could errors exist regardless of whether or not you could accuse something of them? (I wanted to continue on, in any way I could, with questions whose answers it was possible not to arrive at, perhaps because "the question marks weren't placed deeply enough," as someone said.) But was nature really natural? Why were some of the things that humans created not natural? Couldn't it be said, in a broad sense, that everything humans created was also part of nature?

But, as always when I had such thoughts, I failed to obtain answers to the questions over which natural philosophers of old could have agonized. I thought that the earwig which I thought appeared before me at that moment, although it didn't, and placed on my hand and watched as it stayed still, as if dead, after squirming for a while—the earwig, at that moment, represented nature—thoroughly ignored my question. So I became a little angry and wanted to mock and slander nature in any way I could, and thought that a modifier was necessary in order to do so, and said that nature was shabby, false, ashamed, squalid, squalid beyond measure, and above all, cruel beyond measure (I wanted to inflict injustice on nature through an excessive use of adjectives), but as could be easily predicted, I was the one, not nature, who was shabby, false, ashamed, squalid, squalid beyond measure, and above all, cruel beyond measure. So I harbored an ill feeling against nature, and thought that I could expose it without hesitation— I could, in this way, harbor an ill feeling against anything at all, and expose it without hesitation—but I just harbored it without exposing it.

And I looked at the scenes in the landscape, ignoring per- spective with my eyes as I'd done before, as if looking at a paint- ing in which perspective is ignored, and switching around the scenes in the landscape which had become messy in the process, I thought that nature was exposing, almost audaciously, the fact that it was perfectly indifferent to everything that happened to it, or hiding it, through its various faces. I looked around, thinking that there might be something that belonged to nature, a squirrel, for instance, that was watching me in secret as I thought that about nature, but I didn't see anything. Still, I felt as if something were watching me in secret.

But such thoughts seemed dull, and I decided that I wouldn't think anymore. Lying still, I looked up. But as often happens when I'm lying on the grass in a forest, thoughts that seemed trapped in a sort of endless repetition floated around in my mind, and they had a delicate but tenacious feel to them, which made me think that their roots were touching the roots of the grass on which I was lying, that they were taking root in the ground.

As I often do at such times, I tried to fix my gaze on an object so as to break away from tangled thoughts and drive my thoughts to a single point. But there was nothing that held my gaze. I looked around with vacant eyes. Branches were blocking out the sky. Some branches at the top of a tall tree were shaking almost imperceptibly, and the branches, which had nothing really special about them, gave off a very strange, indescribable feeling. It seemed that you would begin to shudder if you looked at them long enough, but I didn't begin to shudder, no matter how long I looked at them. And yet the strange feeling was indescribable indeed, and although I had the feeling, it seemed that the feeling, in the end, couldn't be mine.

Perhaps it was because the tremor of the branches that were shaking so faintly seemed like the waves of a quiet sea, which made it seem as if I were looking up at the surface from under the sea, and as if everything I saw were an underwater scene. At one point, it felt as if the trees were coral reefs, which was a very easy feeling to have, and a feeling that seemed okay to discard, so I discarded the feeling.

Still, in a brief space of time, I let the sun, which was very gradually passing between those branches, and then between those branches and the branches of a neighboring tree, pass very gradually while I was watching it, although it was of course passing as always at a regular interval, and at one point, it looked as if it were caught by the tip of a branch. It was nothing more than a feeling I had, that I was making things up in my mind, but I let myself stay in that state for as long as I wanted.

Peace of mind, which came to me so rarely that when it did come at an unexpected hour it made me feel somewhat awkward and uncomfortable, and led me to keep an eye on it, slightly suspicious because I wasn't unaware that it would soon disappear, came to me like a rain cloud that comes dawdling, but although you couldn't say that it had nothing to do with the peaceful landscape before me, it wasn't just because of the landscape. Peace of mind always came for no good reason, and disappeared for even less of a good reason than when it came.

For quite some time I looked at the branches that gave off an indescribable feeling, and then away from the branches and at the sun which was slowly moving across the vast and boundless sky, and then suddenly leapt to my feet, unbuckled my belt, and began to wrap it around a tree trunk for some reason. I didn't know why I was doing it, but it seemed that it was an okay thing to do. Anyway, the belt fit the tree perfectly, and I was pleased that the girth of the tree was the same as my own. At any rate, the belt was old, and I'd been grappling with the question of how to give it a proper end. (Even after a long time had passed, I thought from time to time about the tree around which I had wrapped a belt, and felt happy to think that somewhere, there was a tree wearing a belt, one of the few trees in the world wearing a belt, perhaps the only one. And it could perhaps stir up the imagination of those who found it.) And indicating that nature should go on doing whatever it was that it was doing, and hoping that nature, which was always silent and seemed impertinent as a result, would stay deeply absorbed in itself for ever after, I gently bent a branch that touched my hand and then let it go, thus bidding nature farewell.

I came out of the forest after that and was walking across the hill where animals were grazing in a herd, but I couldn't tell if they were sheep or goats. The animals, white and gray and black, did not make crying sounds that would identify them as sheep or goats, and there are sheep that look almost like goats, and goats that look like sheep. Perhaps the herd consisted of both goats and sheep. Or there could be a hybrid of a sheep and a goat, although I wasn't sure if such a thing existed, which would look like either a goat or a sheep depending on how you looked at it. It was also possible that some sheep and goats couldn't easily distinguish between goats and sheep, which looked so much like themselves, and suspected that they were of the same species as themselves.

Without really thinking about it, I began to count the animals that I wasn't sure were sheep or goats. But I kept having to start over at ten. The animals, which couldn't possibly know that I was counting them, kept moving around, and the herd kept changing in form although it didn't break off completely (for that was how a herd of sheep maintained its form).

Recalling that when I had trouble falling asleep I counted sheep or other animals, and that I stayed up a whole night once, letting more than five thousand sheep pass through my mind, I thought that counting the animals that were before me, which I wasn't sure were sheep or goats, was different from counting animals when I had trouble falling asleep, but that I wasn't sure what the difference was. Still, I thought that I certainly liked doing something that went on endlessly.

The sun went down over the hill where the animals were

grazing and evening fell, and knowing the pleasure of walking in the evening without saying or thinking anything as mountain shadows lengthened out as much as possible and gradually got buried in darkness and quiet, and everything turned into some kind of an immovable object, I walked in the evening without saying or thinking anything, but pleasure, which seemed on the verge of arising, vanished. If anything, I felt sorrow for no particular reason, a sorrow that might be called the sorrow of evening, whose origin I didn't know, neither to whom it belonged—and I felt that it was the quintessence of all sorrow—which was similar to what you feel when you have a dream that isn't necessarily so sad, about yourself dying, for instance, but makes you stiff, as if paralyzed, with such heavy sorrow upon waking, and it seemed that it had something to do with how I detected a faint trace of sorrow at that moment on the hill that was spread out wide and touching the sky even though it wasn't high. The sorrow I felt at that moment, at least, was a mixture, like all the emotions I felt, of an emotion that was stirred up for good reason at a certain moment, and an emotion that had nothing to do with the moment, which put me at ease even while I was somewhat sad. And the sorrow, along with a certain vagueness there, which seemed infused with nature's languid sigh, something I couldn't put my finger on, made me think again that it was Molloy's town.

And as I walked out of the story I thought of as "Roaming in Molloy's Town" and left the town and rode a train I recalled a memory, a memory of my childhood. In the river that flowed in front of my childhood village, there was a rock called the terrapin rock, named for the terrapins that climbed to the top of the rock and huddled together to bathe in the sun. But what I wanted to think about was not the rock, but a terrapin I saw one day on the meadow. A terrapin had come out of the river, and after taking a walk, or doing its business, it was returning to the river, when it ran into an obstacle, none other than a cow. The cow blocked the terrapin's path, and the terrapin did all it could to return to the river, but the cow, for some reason, was doing all it could to stop it. Did the cow feel a great curiosity about the round thing that was crawling slowly? But the cow had a good reason of its own. The cow pushed around the terrapin with its mouth, and licked the terrapin's shell with its tongue, and then kept licking it, seeing that the slightly salty taste wasn't bad, but the terrapin, which didn't like it, did all it could to escape the cow that was harassing it, to no avail. Things grew worse, for at that moment, two more cows came and joined the cow in licking the terrapin's shell. Surrounded by the three cows, the terrapin tried to slip out through the twelve legs standing like a fence, but it was no use. For a while, the terrapin didn't know where to put itself, and the cows had a good time, and in the end, the terrapin was set free only after the cows lost interest in it, having had their fill of its shell, but it was by now as offended as it could be, so it stretched out its neck and did its best to wipe its own shell with its mouth, to wash away the feel of the cow tongues that had touched it, and at last, began to make its way toward where it had intended to go, or, in other words, the river. In summers I used to climb up to the terrapin rock and dry myself after a swim in the river. When I thought of that, the sorrow I felt on the hill where evening was falling once again seemed groundless, and I scattered what remained of the sorrow out the window into the swiftly passing scenery.

And that night, I went to a city nearby that was somewhat large, where I hadn't planned on going, and went to a club and met a woman of Indian descent, who was born in Madagascar and had moved to France. (Now, having talked about a journey I took in order to see someone in a story, a journey on which nothing happened, I can finally talk about something that has to do with Madagascar, where I've never been and am not sure if I'll ever go.) We had a drink together and chatted in English—she said she was waiting for her boyfriend—after which we somehow ended up dancing—it seemed that she was using me to pass the time until her boyfriend showed up, and I was eager to be used in that way—and said goodbye, touching cheeks lightly as the French do—her boyfriend never showed up—and I took the night train and returned to where I was staying. Anyway, there was something unusual about her, found in unusual animals living only in Madagascar, but I couldn't put my finger on it. She had moved to France when she was young and didn't remember much about Madagascar, and didn't talk much about it, but when I told her about my encounter with a rogue cow around a grazing land somewhere, and how I'd felt tempted to seduce it—the feeling was a mixture of a desire, not unlike the desire to seduce a seductive woman, and a desire that was unlike it, which made it even more complicated—but not knowing how to seduce it—I had nothing to seduce it with, and I couldn't seduce it with myself—and not having considered what to do after seducing it—we could, of course, look into each other's eyes, our eyes having met momentarily, or walk side by side—I stayed with the cow for a little while, and then we each went our way, she showed interest and asked me if I was trying to seduce her, with a pretty smile on her face, and when I told her I wasn't sure, she said that she, too, had once felt tempted to seduce a pretty bird, or even a seductive chair in a furniture showcase. And then she said that the most beautiful scene she had ever witnessed was something she saw as a child, a herd of cattle returning home through baobab trees against a setting sky. I felt as if I could see a little girl driving cattle through baobab trees against a setting sky. But I didn't know what she felt as she drove cattle through baobab trees, or saw someone drive cattle. Half-Indian and half-Caucasian, she seemed like a chameleon to me, and thinking that on the return train, I thought that I might go to Madagascar someday.

At any rate, Madagascar seemed like a decent place to tell someone that you might visit even though you weren't actually going to, and when I was at home by myself, doing nothing, I felt like a chameleon, so when someone asked me why I was thinking about going to Madagascar, I said it was because I wanted to see the chameleons there.

My favorite moments from travels are those that stir or grasp my heart in gentle but strong ways, which make it possible for me to go on traveling. And the things that happen at such moments are actually nothing at all, things that come to light only through those moments, after which they vanish almost without a trace, but remain etched in my subconscious mind, and are in fact more like ordinary things.

A long time ago, I went to Rome, and after checking into a

hotel near the Rome Central Station, from which the Colosseum could be seen—I'd wandered around downtown Rome for a couple of days, but I hadn't felt much of anything—I stayed cooped up in the hotel room for three days, regretting that I'd come to Rome without a particular reason. I spent a long time lying still on the neatly made bed, without unpacking my suitcase or taking my coat off, glaring at a shoddy little replica of the ancient Roman Colosseum on the desk in the room. I wasn't sure what I was doing in Rome, a city of ancient historical sites. Generally, when I was doing perfectly nothing at all, I felt as if I had at least a little idea of I was doing, but that wasn't really the case then. So I thought that doing or not doing something when it didn't matter what you did was certainly different from doing something when you had to do it, a thought that made me wonder if I was thinking right, and I thought that there was everything I needed there, with nothing that wasn't there, and thinking that it didn't really make sense, I went to the Colosseum in the middle of the night and saw stray cats roaming around, and left Rome as if to flee from them.

And I went to New York for several days one cold winter and stayed in the hotel room for most of my time there, and at that time, too, I wasn't sure why I had come to New York and what I wanted there. Feeling a certain kind of comfort in a hotel room that was cleaned every day, removing of all traces of the person who had stayed there the night before, and in which a neutral world of objects was maintained, regardless of the distinctive or indistinctive nature of the room, I took note of what difference that was there, if any, between the perplexity you feel in everyday life and the perplexity you feel in a somewhat unfamiliar place, and dared not go outside, trying to decide if I should plunge uncomfortably or willingly into the somewhat new feeling of perplexity. And I was led to contemplate a thought that wasn't new at all, that the perplexity was a result of the boredom that arises from a vague state in which you don't know what to do, and the awkwardness that arises from a state so comfortable that it makes you shudder.

Looking at the curtains flapping in the open window, I thought that I wouldn't go outside unless a gigantic sailboat, with a full load and the sails taut with wind, entered through the window. So that was the first time I came up with a specific and metaphorical reason for, and tried to justify, staying somewhere doing nothing, feeling so alone, and at the same time, befogged, and much later, on that early morning when a thief tried to break into my house, I felt the same way again. (When traveling, I liked to spend a lot of time looking out the window and watching people pass by, or just staying in the hotel room, not doing anything different from what I did when I was home, and the same was true of the time I stayed cooped up in my room, looking out the window all day and watching flocks of big black birds flying at regular intervals, crying dismally, as I listened to Messiaen's string quartet, which I hadn't heard since I heard it very long ago on the radio, which I normally almost never listened to, but had turned on and kept on because I didn't want to bother turning it off, the morning after being greatly disappointed at a museum exhibiting the works of a famous surrealist painter, which I'd visited the day before, while staying in Brussels for just two days in the middle of one winter.)

And I turned on the television thinking that there were things I could do because I didn't know what it was that I wanted, and while randomly flipping through the channels, I came across a movie. It was a movie called "Trash," directed by Paul Morrissey, who had also worked with Andy Warhol. The movie was one without much of a storyline, in which trashy hippies who spent time mostly in a room, stoned, looking at something or staring off vacantly, or saying or not saying something that did or didn't make sense, did nothing but say trashy things to each other and do trashy things, from the beginning to the end, just as the title indicated— they actually lived off trash, buying drugs with the money they got from selling the trash they picked up. But the movie, which I watched without any expectation, about completely degenerate, lethargic people, and made you feel despondent, was one that showed you how powerful saying nothing could be, and became one of the best movies I've seen.

After watching the movie, I thought once again that living as a Buddhist monk at least once in your life, as most men do in a certain Asian country, or as a hippie for a period in your life, could be something essential in life, that brings out two things that are the most deeply rooted in human nature and are considered polar opposites, but in fact aren't that different from each other.

After that, while watching a program introducing the most skilled tattoo experts in various parts of America, on a channel specializing in tattoos and aired tattoo related programs all day—after I returned from the trip, I wanted to get a tattoo, and although I've decided on what shape and size I want, I haven't gotten one yet because I can't make up my mind as to where on my body I want it—I felt an urge to go outside, but I made a simple, but in its own way big, resolution that I would never go see the Statue of Liberty, one of the things that represented New York—the resolution could be as big as the resolution to visit New York and see all the works in the possession of the Museum of Modern Art—and I was able to keep the resolution.

After spending the day in this way I woke up the next morning, feeling pleased that I hadn't done anything that a first time visitor to New York should do as a matter of course even though I was in New York, and I went to the bathroom and ran a bath in the tub, and while taking a bath, I thought that it might be nice to get a small live octopus and spend time with it in the water. There was a big tub in the bathroom, and it seemed that an octopus would look well in it. The octopus could come out of the bathroom and roam around the room if it wanted, and we could stay in the room together without any regard to each other.

And I thought it would also be nice to wake up from a little nap in a room with an octopus in it, and be lightly, pleasantly surprised upon seeing the octopus on the sofa or the bed. Then I could perhaps take the octopus where it belonged, to the sea. But after finishing my bath, I thought that there were ideas that were good in themselves, but not good for carrying out into action, the idea about an octopus being one of them. Seeing an octopus roam around the room may bring me a light thrill, but the octopus would shudder at the selfish act.

After agonizing for a long time over what to do or what not to do that day, I ended up leaving the hotel without a destination in mind, and followed a sign indicating that there was a park nearby, and arrived at the park in the end. In the park, there were people pushing strollers, people sitting on benches, and people walking, holding hands, as if to say that the park was no different from any other park. But there were also people protesting there, half naked and carrying pickets, people against using animal fur and animal abuse. They were talking about how much people abused animals and getting people's signatures, and although I supported them in my heart, I thought that I couldn't join them in something so meaningful. All I could do regarding all efforts seeking change was sympathize in a detached way from a distance.

I went on walking, leaving behind the people who were against animal abuse, and suddenly, I wanted to go to an amusement park in Coney Island—was it because of a memory of a certain movie that seems quite dull now, or because of the thought I'd had about an octopus?—and took a subway there, but seeing that the gates were firmly shut, although I wasn't sure if it was because it was too late, or because it was winter, I turned away in disappointment—but on the platform at the subway station, I saw a black girl turn round and round to unwrap the long scarf she was wearing while her mother held it by the end, which was very touching, and enough to make up for the disappointment in Coney Island—and returned to my hotel room. No, that wasn't all. Before I did, I wandered around a street in Coney Island that seemed a bit dangerous, and saw a good number of people lined up in the darkness, each carrying a wooden chair somewhere for some reason. I felt very lucky at that moment, because I could imagine, without any grounds, that they were taking them to the night sea to bury them underwater, which was the sort of thing

I wanted to see while traveling, or in everyday life.

Actually, watching the people carrying the chairs simply for some reason, perhaps for an event to be held the next day—no, actually, there were only two black men carrying wooden chairs—I imagined that they could be doing it to calm some monsters that appeared every night in the nearby sea and devoured chairs, and chairs were one of the things in the world that stirred up my imagination. Once I imagined creatures from a planet somewhere in the universe, more intelligent than humans, invading the earth and taking away all its chairs, or visiting the earth for the peaceful purpose of obtaining a few chairs from it, in order to further their research on chairs. When I thought about aliens I imagined aliens on the earth pulling pranks, such as pulling all the screws out of all the things humans have made, or shooting a strange beam to leave only the shadows or outlines of all the life forms on the earth.

And once, I was on my way to a port in the morning to make a reservation on a ship headed to a Scandinavian country, just to go a little further north from Amsterdam, but I suddenly felt no desire to go after seeing a doll drifting down a canal, and decided to give up going to Scandinavia and leave the Netherlands imme-diately—or did the doll come into my sight as I was thinking that I should leave the Netherlands?—but a little thing that happened as I was making my way to the train station led me to stay longer in the Netherlands. I was passing by a bus station when a young Caucasian woman coming toward me smiled at me, no, she was already smiling before she approached me, and asked me cautiously if I could give her two dollars, and the moment she opened her smiling lips wide to say that, I saw, through her uneven teeth— one of the teeth was missing, and another was sticking out—a big chunk of spinach, like a gold tooth someone had put in to show off, in the bright sunlight. And there was a brown stain on her pink blouse, slightly puffed up around her stomach, as if she'd spilled some food on it, and there was some blood on her arm, as if scratched by thorns on a tree, not a lot but a few drops of it, not yet fully congealed. I thought that she must have come before me after stealing spinach from someone's garden at the center of Amsterdam and filling her belly with it, and then making her way through a thorny bush, such as a rosebush.

After thinking for a moment I took out two dollar bills from my wallet and handed them to her, after which I learned that the two dollars I'd given her were a compensation for showing me her teeth, with spinach stuck in between. It also occurred to me that it was because it had been too long since someone had smiled at me without an ulterior motive—even if she did have an ulterior motive, it was for no more than two dollars. She remained standing there smiling, and the somewhat awkward smile wouldn't leave her lips, as if stuck there, as if her facial expression had gotten stuck at the smile. And the smile was something that could be produced only by someone who was captivated by herself, and it seemed that she had long lost interest in the bills she'd received. I took a close look at her face, and everything about her looked funny, the lipstick smeared around her lips, the nose ring she was wearing, the hair that looked as if it had been dyed red, her face itself, the dress with too many flowers on it. She was mumbling something incoherent, and seemed drugged up. I thought a bunch of flowers would suit her, so I wanted to give her a bunch of flowers, but I didn't see any flower shops nearby.

Our encounter was brief, and we parted ways smiling, but thanks to her I could remember the Netherlands as a country in which a woman who smiled, baring her teeth with spinach stuck between them, and had a few little drops of blood on her arm as if scratched by thorns, and had lost her mind, or was drugged up, initiated a conversation with me, and I could stay in the Netherlands for a few more days, feeling refreshed. And during my additional days in the Netherlands, the country seemed almost lovely. It was also because a somewhat strange thing happened while I sat in a café the day before I met her, when a man came up to me and said something in Dutch, and when I told him in English that I didn't understand, he asked me in English if I wasn't a classmate from his school days. When he asked me that, I almost said yes, a little surprised, no, not really surprised, but pretending to be surprised. In the Netherlands, of course, there were a lot of children who were adopted from the East, and he must have taken me for one of his old classmates, and in the end he apologized and left, but that, too, pleased me, and I recalled how once I wondered what it would've been like if I had been adopted into someone's home when I was little, and thought about it briefly. And afterwards, when I met the woman with spinach stuck between her teeth, I couldn't help but feel quite close to her, and the encounter pleased me quite a bit. Such trifling things brought me pleasure, and it was also pleasing to see myself becoming very pleased by such things.

Another time, in a foreign city, Paris, I think, someone asked

me if I weren't from a country in Central Asia, and although I
don't remember how I answered the question at the time, I do
remember that I recalled a country called Turkmenistan, whose
capital's streets, which I saw on television, were lined with massive
new buildings that seemed to embody the socialist ideal, which
I would have been quite satisfied to see if I were Stalin, but were
too empty and deserted, and felt almost surreal, and said that I
was from Turkmenistan, and thought that it was a good thing to
be of ambiguous nationality, and an even better thing to lose your
nationality altogether.

(The things that took place in my life were, like the above,
things that couldn't be called incidents, things that fell short of
being incidents—except, of course, my recent loss of consciousness and collapse at home—things that would turn into nothing
if I didn't fix them in my memory by putting them into writing
like this. By putting into writing the faint, fragile memories in
this way, I'm fixing them, stories that can change again later in a
different way, like printed photographs.)

The next day I returned to the café where I'd met the man
who asked me if I weren't an old classmate and had coffee there,
hoping to see him again, although it would be okay, of course,
not to see him again, and tell him how much his blunder had
pleased me. And I thought I could make a movie, combining the
scenes in Amsterdam in which I met the woman with spinach
stuck between her teeth and the man who mistook me for an
old classmate, with my experiences in New York, as well as things
I experienced or imagined in other places while traveling, because
I felt as if the woman with spinach stuck between her teeth and

the man who mistook me for an old classmate came up to me, like characters in a movie, and posed a riddle and then disappeared, leaving me alone in the movie. It would be a very strange movie without a storyline, whose scenes would linger in the mind despite, or because of, its lack of a storyline. It's a strange thing to dream of making just one movie that's very strange, but it made me happy, as if I were having an enchanting dream. The previous night I'd dreamt about a naked woman whose thighs and chest were embedded with pieces of translucent mother-of-pearl, put together like a mosaic in the form of a woman. I was tangled up naked with the naked woman, which seemed quite erotic. It was an erotic experience that told you that you could have a truly erotic experience only in dreams. And the woman's face was as black as ebony, and naturally led me to think of the word death. I thought I could put that dream, too, in the one movie I could make.

During my additional days in Amsterdam, I mostly sat in a café from which I could see the canal, writing down words such as stained stain, sleeping sleep, dreaming dream, drained drain, and smiling smile. And the words became the phrase, a smiling smile that arises on a drained drain of a stained stain in a dream dreamt by sleeping sleep, upon whose completion I left the Netherlands.

Reading what I've written so far, I think about how I should move forward, or make it move forward, about all its possibilities. It's always a pain to read over what you've written. Writing isn't without moments of joy you can't feel in doing anything else, but such moments are much too rare. And the moments vanish as soon as they come.

It seems now that I am completely lost in what I've written. That was part of my intention, of course, and so it wouldn't be a bad thing to get completely lost in my own story. But getting lost and wandering in a story makes you more clearly aware of yourself as you're disappearing somewhere, in a way that's both similar to but different from getting lost and wandering in a forest or the streets. I feel as if I'm somewhere that doesn't exist, as if I exist somewhere that doesn't exist as a nonexistent being, as if I'm disappearing.

And I feel that this story has already become a failure, in that I tried at first to keep the anecdotes from turning into stories but didn't succeed. But that was expected to a certain extent, and won't be a problem. I may even feel a small private sense of victory in letting this story come, in the end, to a failure.

But still, rambling on—I think that the fact that time is probably the only thing I can waste makes it possible for me to ramble on—is making me very uncomfortable, and even bringing me displeasure that doesn't come with great pleasure, but that's probably something I need to risk as well. Anyway, another problem, although not more serious, is that I'm losing more and more interest in this story I began to write without much ambition, or if such a thing is possible, losing interest I never had in the first place, which is because I have a hard time doing something with an earnest desire, or with a desire disguised as an earnest desire. One of the biggest practical difficulties I have in writing is that too often, I lose interest gradually or suddenly in what I'm writing. But what I've lost interest in is not just this story. I've lost nearly all interest in nearly all things. Perhaps the only thing I have left to do is to write about the slightly interesting process of losing interest in something. Nevertheless, the paradox of writing in order to not write anymore, the paradox that I could write until there's nothing left to write, that it would be difficult not to write until then, will keep me writing.

I have no choice but to keep going, whether I get lost in my story or find my way. I fumble as I write, as if reading Braille, fumbling in my mind. Perhaps I can write without ceasing, as if I didn't care, somewhat carelessly, because I'm not genuinely interested. For there's a kind of interest you can show because you're not genuinely interested, a kind of concern you can show because you're not genuinely concerned, for there are such things. I could probably go on writing this, for I know too well that it is perhaps perfectly useless.

If the purpose of travel, in a way, is to shatter illusions about an unknown world, my travels are true to their purpose in that respect. A logic could be developed, a logic that's perhaps forced, that it's best not to travel at all in order to maintain an illusion, and in fact, when I considered traveling, I was always conflicted between maintaining an illusion by not traveling, and seeing an illusion get shattered by traveling. I feel the same way about Turin, which I felt an urge to visit at one point, which brings the dilemma of whether to go to Turin, a city where the illusions I had about it were sure to get shattered the moment I set foot there, and see my illusions surely get shattered, or not go there and maintain my illusions. Perhaps the dilemma could be solved by maintaining my illusions for a while by not going to Turin for some time yet in the future, and then going there and seeing them get shattered.

I don't feel much of an interest in majestic historical relics that show traces of time, or beautiful and impressive natural objects. Rarely did a place or a structure I actually saw surpass what I saw on television or in a photograph. I've almost never been moved by a place or a structure the way you should be moved. The Heidelberg Castle, which looked picturesque in a photograph, moved me so little, if at all, when I actually went there one summer that I couldn't believe my eyes—at least, I was much less moved by the castle than I was by the sight of a black girl spinning around to extricate herself from her long scarf as her mother held on to the end—and the same went true for the old Hindu ruins in an Asian jungle that was very moving. The reason why a certain place or structure looked all right on television or in a photograph was because I could contemplate some interesting thoughts I had while looking at them.

I left behind the Heidelberg Castle and went to see the Neuschwanstein Castle, another famous old castle in Germany, and I liked it much more when I hadn't actually seen it, shrouded in mist and surrounded by Bavarian coniferous forests, and standing tall at the top of a steep mountain in a fortress-like atmosphere. And that was because I left the mist-shrouded castle after learning some facts surrounding the castle, such as that the man who built the castle was Ludwig II, who was fascinated by Wagner and sponsored him, and identified himself with the mythical German heroes of Wagner operas and had himself painted to look like them, and was so handsome that he looked like a hero, and liked swans so much that he had all the door handles decorated with a swan motif, and liked to go around in the nude, and died in a lake near the castle, although it's unclear whether the death was a suicide or a homicide.

I was able to swim for a little while in the lake below the Neuschwanstein Castle, whose water was so cold that it would be difficult to dip your foot in it even in the middle of summer, and then take a nap while drying off, which was an experience that more than made up for the disappointment at the Heidelberg Castle. And while sleeping, I had a dream that I had joined a sort of guerilla movement and was in a fierce battle against an unknown enemy in the far off Amazonian jungle in Bolivia, but there was something that gave me a harder time than fighting in the jungle, which was none other than fighting back the diarrhea that was about to explode, and in the end I woke up and actually relieved myself with urgency in the forest. I could see why I had a dream about getting diarrhea, but not why I had a dream set in the Amazonian jungle in Bolivia, when I was at a lake surrounded by the forest near the Neuschwanstein Castle.

Many times I've been to a certain place where I couldn't see anything because it was shrouded in mist, and each time I felt very lucky on the whole. For in some places with thick mist, I didn't need anything, just the mist.

One winter when I went to Venice and arrived at St. Mark's Square the mist was so thick that, to exaggerate a bit, I couldn't even see the bag I was carrying, and, to exaggerate a bit more, I couldn't even see my hand that was holding the bag, and to exaggerate some more, I couldn't even see myself—a voice inside me says that a story like this should be exaggerated, and then exaggerated some more, but I'm ignoring it now—and in the end, the only part I saw of St. Mark's Basilica, facing the square, was the entrance. Nevertheless, I saw a blue balloon in the air, tied to a string in the hand of a child being led out of the entrance by his mother, which made quite an impression on me. I could have taken a look inside the basilica but there were too many people, and in the end, I stood in St. Mark's Square, which Napoleon called the finest drawing room in Europe, and saw the belfry next to the basilica, which was rebuilt after it collapsed in the early twentieth century, although I didn't see a spire which I may have been able to see if I climbed up the steep staircase and if there was a spire, although I don't know if there was a spire on the basilica, and saw the bottom of the belfry as I recalled a story surrounding the belfry, about how a cat was crushed to death when the belfry collapsed, and, suddenly, I recalled a thought I once had, without any grounds, a thought that seemed even more plausible because it was without any grounds, that cats may have been the first victims of the French Revolution, and that there must have been many other revolutions and wars whose first victims were cats or other animals.

And in the Venetian mist, which offered almost nothing of a view, I suddenly became curious as to what happened to the animals in zoos around the world in the midst of confusion such as revolutions or wars. I wondered if the cages were bombed or destroyed, and if some animals died and others survived and ran out to the streets, exposing themselves to the strange wild world of humans in which they couldn't receive any kind of protection, and if some of them went mad, unable to adapt to the strange environment, and starved to death while roaming the streets like a madman. I wondered if among them was a lion that, momentarily blinded by the headlights of an oncoming car, leapt in front of the car, and a gorilla that got on a subway train, and a rhinoceros that ran across a bridge and jumped over the guardrail, and a zebra that entered a basement pub that was still open even amid the confusion, and not knowing what to do among the startled people, ended up sitting on a stool, and a horse that accompanied the zebra into the pub, for which someone poured a beer, recalling that horses liked beer, and an ostrich that went into a restroom in a restaurant, frightening a woman freshening her makeup after doing her business, and a badger that climbed up the stairs in a building that was half destroyed through bombing, and a stork that came flying into someone's kitchen and sat on the table, and a pelican that hatched an egg in a bedroom whose owner had fled. (Surreal situations that could take place when war actually broke out were something I liked to imagine, because they could cause rifts in my everyday perceptual experience, although they didn't make me want to experience war.)

The fate of zoo animals in the midst of confusion was a somewhat strange thing to think about in mist-shrouded Venice, which is why it struck my fancy, and I wondered if there was a zoo in Venice, the city of water, and I thought that it might be nice to go to the zoo, if there was one, and listen to the cries of the animals that couldn't be seen in the mist, but I wanted to keep the thought as only a thought (I still wonder if there's an ordinary zoo in Venice, or just huge aquariums).

And while having a very leisurely meal at a restaurant in

mist-shrouded St. Mark's Square, and listening to the sound of the bell from the belfry of the basilica, which seemed to break everything into very little pieces, I became lost in some rambling thoughts that come to my mind when I'm having a very leisurely meal, and I suddenly wondered if there was a trampoline in a park or a playground in Venice, with children jumping up and down on it in a thick mist, and thought it would be nice if there were such children. If you jumped on a trampoline in a mist in which you couldn't see anything, you could feel as if you were jumping up and down in a cloud. Perhaps I was led to think such a thought because I saw a blue balloon, tied to a string in the hand of a child being led out of St. Mark's Basilica by his mother, floating in the air just before that. I thought it would be nice to jump ropes in such a thick mist and tried to picture myself jumping ropes without much success.

After the meal, I sat listening for a little while to the cooing of pigeons that moved like phantoms, like the ghosts of some animals in the mist, and then left Venice earlier than I'd planned, which strangely made me feel that I could have a special feeling for the city, by not experiencing anything more there. I actually stayed in Venice for no more than a few hours, so it seemed that I saw or felt something that I couldn't see or feel when I saw the city of water with plenty of time on my hands. At least by doing so I could think, in mist-shrouded Venice, about what kind of a fate the zoo animals met amid confusion, and about jumping on a trampoline in a mist, and perhaps I could tell someone about it, and enjoy seeing him misunderstand, or only partially understand, what I was saying.

In the end, all I did in Venice was imagine, in a mist-shrouded square, what happened to zoo animals amid confusion, and see a blue balloon—a blue balloon in a mist is not a sight to be easily seen anywhere—tied to a string in the hand of a child being led by his mother, and I asked myself if I could say that I'd been to Venice, with that, and as soon as I asked, I answered that I could. I went to Venice again later, but I didn't enjoy it as much as I did on my first visit. I went to St. Mark's Square again, but I didn't enter the basilica. Nevertheless, I checked to see that St. Mark's Basilica was in the baroque style, and didn't have the spire of a gothic basilica I pictured in my mind. And I saw many balloons in the hands of children in the square, but they were just ordinary children's balloons. Nevertheless, I learned that at one time in Venice, masked balls were so popular that the people of Venice went around wearing masks for half the year. In the end, masked balls were banned by law due to all the scandalous things people did hiding behind masks, but it was pleasant to imagine people wearing masks, wandering in the mist like ghosts, in the city of mist which itself was wearing a mask.

To add to the feeling of being lost and wandering in my own story, I recall memories of places I've been to and hover above them like a phantom. A memory from Paris comes to the phantom's mind.

At the time, I was spending most of my time doing nothing in a hotel room from which the top of the Eiffel Tower, which could be seen from almost anywhere in downtown Paris, could be seen through a window. I'd wanted a room as high up as possible, but ended up getting a room on the middle floor. In that room, I had a quarrel, more violent than necessary, with the woman I was traveling with at the time, for a reason that's unclear now, no, a reason that was unclear even then, a reason that seemed absurd when you thought about it for a moment, and much too absurd when you thought about it for a while—the reason, it seemed, could be found out if I tried to find it out, but I wanted to remain in ignorance if possible, and wanted to feign ignorance. We stayed cooped up in that room for two days in a poor state, utterly exhausted. I wanted to get out of there, but it seemed that I couldn't find the right moment. I suggested that she wash herself, and she did so without a fuss. I made the suggestion because I had a sudden picture of her shampooing her hair, which was because I'd stepped out for a moment that day and bought a balsamic shampoo at a shop, and the reason why I bought the shampoo was because of its brand name, which I've now forgotten. She went to the bathroom to wash herself, and in the meantime, I thought it might be well to leave while she was in the shower shampooing her hair, and packed my things. And I opened the bathroom door and quietly watched her naked body in the shower for a moment, then left the hotel. That was the last I saw of her, and how I wanted to remember her, and how I do remember her, and so she remains a good memory for me.

Having checked into another hotel, I had to deal with a sense of betrayal about the woman who must be dealing with a sense of betrayal upon finding me gone while drying her hair after a shower, so I took out from my coat pocket the small Eiffel Tower replica she'd bought for me at a shop the day before, made up of pieces of wood glued together, and broke it into small pieces, put the pieces back in my pocket, and went outside with a heavy heart, and it happened to be raining, which made my heart even heavier, so I went to a nearby restaurant with an even heavier heart. At the restaurant I ordered something that couldn't really be identified, which contained a lot of boiled carrots, which I hate, and I ate halfheartedly, absorbed in picking out the pieces of carrot without hiding my hostility toward boiled carrots, and arranged the pieces into the word "NO," but I wasn't sure what I was saying no to.

When I went out of the restaurant I was still hungry, but it seemed that I had no emotion left in me that should be dealt with after breaking up with a woman. Nevertheless, I threw away the Eiffel Tower replica in my pocket piece by piece here and there as I walked, and hoped that the woman I'd broken up with would live a difficult life that suited her.

I returned to the hotel after wandering around the streets and felt the surge of emotions that come over you when you're alone in a room just after a breakup, and thought that for a while now, mostly when I was suddenly awake, I'd be feeling an extreme sorrow weighing down upon me, though it came from far away, and then the sorrow would gradually fade away, which seemed to be the sad thing about breakups. And I tried to think about a more real problem—for instance, I didn't have very much money left, and had to think about the problem of getting home—but nothing seemed real. Outside, where it was raining, a fierce wind was blowing erratically, and it seemed that the sound of the wind knocking at the window was mocking and picking on every thought I had, my very being. I felt an urge to go home and sit on my sofa in the living room, caressing the fabric sofa with my hand to savor being home, and sit vacantly, feeling the texture of the sofa, as I do sometimes after returning from a trip.

Nevertheless, amid a vague feeling of loneliness and frustration, which gently washed over me, I became seized with a strange feeling, and made a somewhat strange resolve that I wouldn't even go near the Eiffel Tower, which I couldn't help but see out the window—the Eiffel Tower could be seen from there as well—as if by doing so I could keep myself from falling even deeper into the distress I was in. I didn't have anything against the Eiffel Tower, a massive steel-frame structure. The Eiffel Tower was a public historical heritage that was much too famous, and it was difficult to have personal feelings about it, just as it was difficult to have personal feelings about the Egyptian sphinx. No, to be precise, you could have personal feelings about them somehow, in some way, it was quite possible—just as it was possible to have personal feelings about certain things in your house, for instance, a damaged chair with a broken leg, a chipped kitchen knife, or your sock, which you discovered had a hole in it—but it was difficult to express those feelings.

I came to have personal feelings about the Eiffel Tower because I could see the Eiffel Tower out the window the whole time we were quarreling, and I was as tired of seeing the Eiffel Tower as I was of having a long quarrel with her, and grew angrier at the Eiffel Tower than I was at her, and in the end, I was glaring at the Eiffel Tower like someone learning to express a certain kind of anger. It seemed that the Eiffel Tower out the window, soaring high into the sky, was urging me to come to a decision, as if to egg us on to fight, without helping me come to a decision, and it also seemed that everything in the city wanted us to break up. A storm was raging outside as if on cue, as if a huge animal were showing discomfort, a storm that was like a huge animal in itself. And at one point, a bright light that shone in through the window seemed to inflict a wound, almost, like a rock that broke a windowpane and came flying in.

And I hated everything about Paris, which had become the stage for our breakup, even though it wasn't responsible for our breakup, and I felt that my resentment was justified. I wanted to leave Paris as soon as possible but couldn't easily do so, perhaps because I thought that the woman I'd broken up with may still be somewhere in Paris.

And there was a certain banality in the Eiffel Tower, the symbol of Paris, which could be seen out the window, a banality that was in everything, which could be found if you looked for it, and I felt the same way about Paris when I left the hotel and wandered around downtown. But it wasn't just because I was in a poor condition that everything looked poor in my eyes. Everything has its own inherent banality, and I saw such banality in Paris, a city of great cultural heritage. (Writing about a terrible trip I took, as I'm doing now, brings me a strange sort of pleasure. And I watch my pleased self as if I'm watching someone else, confirming once again that I'm a strange person who's pleased by strange things, which pleases me.)

That night, taking a bath in my exhaustion, I looked at the Eiffel Tower, thinking for a moment about the nature of banality that could be found in an object itself, or in a consciousness interacting with an object, then fell asleep in the bathtub, and had a dream that I was rolling a ball that grew larger or smaller, on a tiny star that, too, continued to grow larger or smaller, and had great difficulty rolling the ball when the star grew even smaller than the ball, which wasn't a nightmare but gave me a hard time as I dreamt, but when I woke up, I felt nothing, nothing at all indeed, and I thought that the reason why it was difficult for me to have a lasting relationship with someone was because it was difficult for me, even when I met someone and continued to see her, to find a reason to keep seeing her, and thought that perhaps the ball in the dream represented my thoughts. And yet it wasn't easy for me to find a reason to break up with someone, either, which made it difficult for someone to keep seeing me, as well as break up with me.

Nevertheless, for some reason, I went to the Eiffel Tower area the next day, and snuck my way into a group of tourists and listened for a moment to the guide's explanation, and in the end, I tried to climb the massive steel tower—perhaps because of the long queue under the tower, made up of people who wanted to climb it, which gradually grew shorter but seemed as if it would never give you a turn, and perhaps I just wanted to stand in the queue without thinking about anything—but when I was almost at the ticket booth after waiting in the long queue, I broke away from it, again for some reason, a reason that may or may not have been reasonable, and then queued up again, once again for some reason—I was making an effort not to climb the Eiffel Tower, which seemed to be beckoning at me with effort, telling me to climb up its body—and when it was my turn, I left the queue like someone who had changed his mind at the last minute, and vowed that I would never come near the Eiffel Tower again, and left the area and checked into another hotel from which, of course, a part of the tower could be seen. I thought of the museums I'd visited on my previous trip to Paris, but I didn't want to see any paintings this time.

As I lay in bed looking at the Eiffel Tower, which could be seen only in part through the hotel window, I once again had a vague thought that there are certain scenes, objects, that you can see freely at last when they're seen only in part, and that there are moments in which a part of something becomes equal to the thing itself, although it doesn't surpass the thing. And I thought that the reason why I didn't climb the Eiffel Tower wasn't because I had lost my nerve at seeing the massive tower, which could be seen only in part through the window at that moment, but which stood in stately glory when seen from just below. What did make me lose my nerve, for no reason, was the statue of a peeing boy I saw in Brussels.

In the hotel room I felt uncomfortable looking at the Eiffel Tower, which could be seen only in part through the window, and which reminded me that I was in Paris, and at one point, I leapt up from the bed and ran to the window as if in a race, and closed and opened the curtains several times, repeating the act until the scene out the window looked resigned, and, in the end, I closed the window and the curtains completely so that it could no longer be seen. And then I had the sudden thought that a part of the top of the tower that could be seen from my house, one of the symbols of the city in which I lived, could be seen from my bedroom window, and I felt at ease, thinking that I was in a hotel somewhere in the world. I lay still in bed, listening to the sound of quiet footsteps of people passing through the corridor from time to time, which the carpet absorbed, and when the sound faded away and silence fell again, I mumbled some words that sounded like footsteps.

And at one point I took out the map of downtown Paris I got from the tourist information office, and put a candle flame to the spot I assumed to be the hotel I was staying at and made the small flame spread out in a circle, swallow some areas here and there in downtown Paris, and, in the end, turn the map into ashes, rendering downtown Paris void. And looking at the faint circle of light, created by the candle flame that had set all of Paris ablaze, I came up with the expression "corrupt light." And I thought of Kafka, who died a terribly painful death due to laryngeal tuberculosis at a sanitarium in Austria—for at the time I was on the last page of a thick compilation of his letters—and pictured myself pacing around the sanitarium courtyard for a moment, looking at the window of the room where Kafka must be dying, and at one point the sanitarium overlapped with the Parisian hotel in which I was staying, for I was coughing severely, like a tuberculosis patient, from a cold I'd caught earlier.

Looking at the ordinary wallpaper in the hotel room in which I was staying, I briefly considered death in a hotel room in a foreign land, which I'd always considered, and how a hotel room was a good place in which to have such a thought. But taking my own life still seemed premature, and I thought about suicide only in a vague and faint way.

And I recalled the time several years earlier when I went to

France and stayed in a small town with no clear purpose or reason, in order to leave the country where I was born and lived in because I couldn't stand almost anything about it.

When I thought of the small town, someone always came to my mind before anything else. In a little square in that French town I stayed in there was a statue of someone who was a scientist as well as a cyclist, and a beggar who was the spitting image of Karl Marx always sat next to it at a certain hour. But the beggar, at whose side was a bag which looked as if it would contain *The Communist Manifesto,* didn't do anything at all, as if he had forgotten his duty as a beggar, or as if he were doing his duty as a beggar. I'd never seen a beggar who didn't do anything, not to that extent. It seemed that the man, who looked questionable as a beggar, carried out his routine activities such as eating or receiving alms in other places, and his spot next to the statue seemed to be a place he visited in order to not do anything. No, it's not true that he didn't do anything at all. He did one thing, which was to take out some kind of a candy from his pocket at a certain time of the day, take off the plastic wrapping and put the candy in his mouth, and suck on it quietly like someone lost in meditation, and when he did, it seemed as if the present world, whose ideals haven't been realized, were quietly, sweetly crumbling away. No, this isn't true. He didn't do anything at all, not even suck on a candy. It was my imagination that put a candy in his mouth. That didn't suit him. He was better off doing nothing, which, fortunately, was what he was doing. In that town, where I saw a dolphin tube float down the river one winter, or which I left, thinking I saw a dolphin tube floating down the river, I dated a French woman for several months, and we would drive to nearby castles in her little car, and take walks in the woods, or hold each other in the woods, smelling the grass and talking, or taking a nap. One day, awake from one of those naps in the woods, I saw her, still in her sleep, and suddenly felt as if my life were happening out of my hands, which felt pleasant beyond description, which made me smile, and she, awake now, asked me the why I was smiling. When I didn't tell her the reason, she didn't pry, and I said it would be nice if we could come like this more often and take naps, and we did so several more times. And I would go see her on the bicycle she lent me, and the handlebars of the old bicycle were slightly turned to the left, so in order to go in a straight line, I had to mentally turn them slightly to the right, and do so in reality. Anyway, one day, I found that the bicycle, which I'd placed in a park, was gone. Someone had brutally severed the chain and taken the bicycle. We didn't go around looking for the lost bicycle, but for several days after that whenever we sat in cafes we would stare fixedly at passing bicycles, and she said that her bicycle was easily recognizable. I felt as if she were saying that she could recognize her own baby, so I felt it imperative that we find the bicycle. But finding a lost bicycle was harder than finding a lost baby, and we never did find the bicycle. And we seriously discussed stealing someone's bicycle, but we didn't actually commit theft. Still, we kept our eyes on bicycles when we took walks, and all the bicycles were brutally chained up. I don't remember much else about her, but I do remember that thanks to her I learned French very quickly, and that she made me feel awkward by crying when I left the city. I awkwardly took her hand and tried to respond in a way you should in front of someone crying, but it wasn't easy. Fortunately, she didn't seem to notice that I felt awkward, because she was busy crying. With that, I could sum up what happened between us. (It may be wrong to talk about your relationship with someone, short or long, and furthermore, about someone's life, in such a way, but everything can be summed up in a few sentences.)

In the end, I came out of the hotel, and before leaving Paris, went again, for some reason, to the Eiffel Tower area that I'd vowed never to go near again and sat with my back to the tower on a bench from which the tower could be seen in its entirety, and, seeing the person sitting on the bench next to mine staring off into space, I, too, stared off into the space into which he was staring, but then he suddenly turned away his gaze, as if angry at discovering that someone was looking at something he alone was looking at, something that he alone should look at—I couldn't understand the reason at all, for the space into which he was staring was an exceedingly blue sky with no clouds at all, and there being no signs of weather change, it seemed that the space, in which there was nothing but the blue sky, wouldn't change at all no matter how he stared at it, no matter how much he stared at it—and glared at me, which made me realize that space, which I thought was for everyone, and something at which anyone could look at any time, wasn't something at which you could look thoughtlessly at anytime, that there was something in space that people shouldn't look at together. No, I think it was more because I had a hangover and was quite red in the face. But looking with such disapproval at someone who was red in the face because of a hangover was something that no human should do. I turned my gaze to something else, and saw a black dog. It would be very big when full grown, but it was still small. The dog didn't yet possess the dignity that dogs of that breed have when full grown. In a little while a white dog—it was a kind that doesn't grow to be very big, and was small, although it was already an adult dog—appeared, and the two felt each other out for a moment, then sniffed at each other and barked. The dogs seemed to be communicating perfectly with each other. Then in a moment, the white dog went off somewhere else, and the black dog, left alone, went to a flower-bed nearby and ran around among the flowers playfully, wantonly. The dog, like all dogs, demonstrated that dogs want to run around every chance they get, and never miss an opportunity to do so. At that moment it suddenly occurred to me that one night, while spending the night with the woman I'd broken up with, I might have strangled her at one point when it seemed as if I would pass out. I was drunk, and extremely tired, and it seemed that I unwit-tingly strangled her with my hands, then came to myself when it looked as if she had stopped breathing and let go, and woke her up by slapping her cheeks several times. But it wasn't clear if such a thing had actually happened.

In the flowerbed, there were roses and other pretty flowers of various colors, and I casually hoped in secret that the dog would trample on the flowers even while being pricked by their thorns, as if it couldn't help itself, and thoroughly ruin the flowerbed. But the dog was careful in its own way not to ruin the flowers, although it didn't look as if it would be, and wasn't injured by the thorns hidden by the trees, either.

Thinking about how many different breeds dogs and cats have

developed into, and how nice it would be if someday humans would do so as well, I thought again about the woman I'd broken up with, and thought that it was for the good of both of us that we broke up, and pictured the day when humans would have evolved into as many different breeds as there are of dogs and cats, and thought, as to the breakup, that we had merely found one of the countless reasons for which we should break up. Perhaps the reason why we broke up was because I couldn't find a reason to keep seeing her, and I thought such a reason was sufficient for a breakup. And I thought that everything that can happen in the world only happens because it can, that what happens is just that something among the things that can't happen loses its possibility of not happening—everything that has happened up to this point could have not happened—that if there is a purpose to the world, it's to make everything that can happen, happen. And I thought, as if coming to a conclusion, that my mind was made up while I was looking at a part of the massive steel structure called the Eiffel Tower out the window, and that I, having always pictured the end of my relationship with someone, had always pictured where and how my relationship with her would come to an end. And it seemed that the fact that I thought about her for a moment told me nothing as to if I still had feelings for her, or if the opposite were true, and that's what I believed.

Looking at the Eiffel Tower, I tried to savor the pleasure a breakup brings—in the same way I sought some pleasure in returning home from a trip, looking at the empty house with no one there, and feeling that I was back to my original self, or in other words, my lone self—but without success.

I had already had a chance to break up with her before that. Late one night when we were in the city where we lived, we were sitting in a cafe, and she was telling me that she was breaking up with me. I'd already felt earlier that something between us had come to an end, and I wondered why the feeling that something had come to an end always came to me before something actually came to an end, and I quietly listened to her, thinking that perhaps it was because I always had in me a sense of anticipation for the end of something. Anyway, while it was raining, and while she was talking, a man who had been passing by outside the window came to a stop and looked at the window, and it turned out that he was someone I knew. I waved lightly at him when she stopped talking for a moment and looked elsewhere, but he didn't seem to see us inside. He went off somewhere else after a little while, staggering as if drunk, but when I looked out the window a moment later, he was once again passing in front of it. For several minutes even after that, he kept going back and forth as if lost, or for some other reason, like an illusion, and I had a hard time focusing on what she was saying because of him, and accepting what was happening to me as something that was actually happening to me, and although it wasn't necessarily because of that, we couldn't break up that night.

I recalled some memories I had of her, for instance, how we picked acacia flowers together every spring and made liquor with them, and how she was always more daring than I was in every way, and how we talked about the fact that we didn't have a single picture of one of us sitting and the other lying with his or her head on the other's leg, against the backdrop of a landscape, and how I thought that we may never end up having a picture like that, although one of us said that he or she wanted a picture like that, and I felt a little sad thinking about the process and the results involved in meeting and breaking up with someone, in which the person seems indispensable at times when you're seeing each other, but becomes irrelevant after you break up, and in the end, becomes almost completely removed from your mind, as if the person had never existed, but the sadness, too, like the joy that seems insufficient to be called joy even when I do feel joy, seemed insufficient to be called sadness, and I didn't feel anything more special than that. One of my biggest problems was that I couldn't feel any emotion fully. I must have come across something beautiful once, and felt that it was beautiful, if only in that moment, there must have been such a moment, but I didn't have a clear memory of such a moment.

Looking at the Eiffel Tower I'd tried so hard not to see, I felt a sort of confidence rise in me, confidence that I'd fail in all my future relationships as well, although I didn't know where the confidence came from, and thought that I could put a closure to our relationship by writing something about how I met and broke up with her, perhaps a novel about a relationship that turned into a failure, or never turned into a romantic relationship—thinking that sometimes, all you can do about something that's come to an end is talk about it—and felt somewhat tempted to write a love story, but writing such a thing seemed a very unseemly thing to do. Anyway, a little while after we broke up, I saw her, no, someone who looked very much like her, walking side by side on the street with a man, holding hands, looking affectionate, and realized that

I'd never walked with her like that, holding hands—I always felt awkward walking with a woman, holding hands, and offered my hand grudgingly as if I were about to shake off her hand—and thought that the fact could explain one aspect of my romantic relationships, and that perhaps I could write a story about that, but again I gave up.

I was deeply disappointed by the game the dog was playing, and in the end got up from the bench, went to a nearby park, and sat on an empty swing, picturing the playground near my house that I visited from time to time, and thought that I might be able to go home with a happy heart if I saw girls jumping ropes, or a dog being dragged away by someone against its will, past children running around columns of water spurting from the ground— once I went somewhere and saw someone climb an artificial rock wall in a park in the city and sincerely hoped that he would fall in the middle of climbing, and could end my journey and come home when, in the end, he fell to the ground—but there were no such sights to be seen. There were, however, children running around between columns of water spurting straight up in a nearby fountain, but the sight, which ordinarily may have drawn a different response from me, made me feel indifferent at that moment. But I was pleased to see instead a girl sitting on a bench eating ice cream. The ice cream in her hand was melting and trickling down her hand, and it was always pleasant to see a child licking melting ice cream. Was it because the ice cream was trickling down a child's hand? Or did ice cream trickling down any hand bring me pleasure? Or did the pleasure come from my idea of ice cream melting in hand? I can't be sure.

And by then I was feeling somewhat ridiculously good after passing a period of extreme bitterness resulting from the breakup, so I tried to make my somewhat ridiculously good mood ridiculously better, or keep it up, at least, but it wasn't easy, and there was nothing around me that responded to my effort.

A Caucasian man who looked somewhat slow was sitting on a bench next to me, and I saw that he was plucking his nose hair very subtly, in his own way, as if he weren't doing such a thing as plucking nose hair, as if he were concerned with what people around him thought, although he didn't seem concerned, and what he was doing looked so subtle yet naïve that it made those who were watching him feel extremely frustrated. He somehow managed to pluck a few strands of his nose hair, and although it was quite understandable that he was concerned about not having plucked the rest, it was very unseemly that he was plucking his nose hair like that, while pretending not to, in a public place. He could have gone someplace without people and plucked the rest of his nose hair as much as he wished, to his heart's content, but he didn't. Plucking your nose hair in a public place like that should be legally banned, just as it's legally banned to name or call a pig Napoleon in France. Seeing someone plucking his nose hair could make you aware of your own nose hair, even if it didn't make you pluck your nose hair, which could stop your train of thought.

Anyway, at that moment, a woman with long blond hair, who had brought with her a girl with long blond hair, looked with disapproval at this man from the East, who looked dazed and yet was glaring threateningly at everything in his sight for no apparent reason, taking up the swing that was for her blond girl—there was another swing next to me, but it was broken—and glared at me, waiting for me to get off the swing. Her gaze wasn't insufferable, but in the end, I got off the swing and went off to a side. I was used to quietly making way or sidestepping for people who wanted a certain spot in a place.

Glaring at the swing and the girl who now had her feet on the swing, soaring up into the sky with her long hair flying prettily in the air, I thought that it would be nice if the swing magically flew high up into the sky to a place of no return with the girl still on it, and thought that it was quite amusing to watch a girl who looked as if she would fly away, while hoping that she would fly away.

But I went somewhere else, thinking that the woman who was still glancing at me could report me to the police, and suddenly decided to go all the way to the Versailles Palace, for some reason, but it was so boring there that I became sullen and wanted to take revenge on the palace, which had done nothing wrong. A pleasant, overwhelming feeling, which comes at times from a structure taking up enormous space, did not come from the Versailles Palace. Nothing but arrogance could be seen in the Versailles Palace, which looked stiff on the whole and seemed as if it would never look otherwise, which was boring.

What I thought of while looking at the Versailles Palace, where everything was in perfect balance, were the people of the royal family and the aristocrats who had strolled there in the past in fancy but uncomfortable clothing, and although I had nothing against them, I felt a strong urge to do something outrageous, to pull off such a thing, to make some kind of an unreasonable demand, and it wasn't so much because I felt that a king of France, who was holding a fan in the brochure on Versailles in my hand, was fanning the urge—I only imagined this, and there was no king of France holding a fan in the brochure, but still, I pictured Louis XVI suddenly opening up his beautiful fan with an exotic painting on it to startle his favorite cat (I wonder what the cat's name was), and playing around with the cat, for every king, and everyone, must, at times, want to think playful thoughts or play around, and actually think playful thoughts or play around—but because in watching people moving around in groups and flocks of pigeons walking on the ground or flying in the air, which made it seem as if everything were in motion—a baby near me was trying to catch an ant on the ground, with a hand that was suitably small for catching ants, but, being clumsy, he was doing so without success—I felt an urge to direct myself at something static, to make the scene come to a stop, at which moment I happened to see swans in the palace pond, and it suddenly occurred to me that I could make that happen by throwing a stone at one of them and hitting it. Or perhaps I felt an urge to create a small stir in the surface of the pond, which was quietly reflecting a brilliantly sunny and peaceful day, regardless of the swans.

But because of the people around me, I couldn't do to the swans what you shouldn't do to swans. Nevertheless, I ended up bearing somewhat playful, casual malice toward the swans, which wasn't because I wanted to commit a casual act of evil or atrocity, going along with the popular belief that travel sets you free.

I had nothing against swans, just as I had nothing against the royal family and the aristocrats of France. If I did have anything against them, I could have done something on that pretext. Still, as I walked the paths through the impeccably manicured garden during my few hours of stay at Versailles, I couldn't help but be afflicted by the thought that I should do something to the swans. Perhaps the thought came from the ill feeling I'd been harboring toward the French for some time. It seemed to me that they were excessively proud of their culture, to the point of conceit. It was easy, of course, to have your pride of something turn into conceit, which was understandable, but it seemed that the pride of the French seemed to go to such a ridiculous degree as to support the idea that pride was suppose to be ridiculous.

Some ideas are difficult to shake off because the temptation to surpass them and make them materialize is too great, for they can't be confined in the mind because they're ridiculous, and the more ridiculous they are, the larger they become, which was the case for my idea of doing something to the swans.

And, as I considered the idea, it seemed that the swans that were peacefully swimming or sitting still, indifferent to all the problems and cares of the world, in the palace pond of an old French king, were a symbol of monarchy, and that doing something to the swans would be a useless act of defiance against monarchy. Monarchy has long disappeared, and so it seemed that I was too late in defying it, but it seemed that I was fighting something that didn't exist, this thing called monarchy, and that doing something to the swans, a symbol of monarchy, was my own lone and belated struggle against monarchy, and I'd be able to taste the joys and sorrows of the struggle by myself.

It seemed that it could be fun to be arrested by the French police, in the event that I hit a swan in the palace pond of an old French king and made it swoon or die, and have a French newspaper print a small article on a foreigner from the East who incurred the anger of the sensible people of France by hurting or killing, with no reason at all or with a clear objective, one of the elegant swans long beloved by the royal family, the aristocrats, and the people of France. And it seemed that it wouldn't be so bad to be in the paper for something like that. Perhaps I could be arrested by the police and make false statements to my own disadvantage, or plead the Fifth and say nothing to the end, thinking to myself that what I did was express anger on behalf of all the immigrants and foreign residents who have been persecuted and are still being persecuted in the country of liberty, equality, and fraternity, and then go to a French jail or be deported. Once that occurred to me, I felt strongly tempted to carry it out into action. At that moment I was fully ready to pay the price for a misdeed I hadn't even yet committed and saw it as a necessary step that criminals must take. But it was something that required great courage, and entailed the very tiresome process of repeated failures until actually hitting a swan and making something happen to it, and it was for that reason that it was difficult for me to carry out in reality. Still, although I was tired and exhausted from the midday heat of summer, I kept on thinking that I should, not submitting to it, in a way, commit an atrocious act of some kind. But it helped to have had my fill of such undesirable thoughts about swans. By having various thoughts about swans, I could keep myself from actually doing something to them. Thinking a lot about something was a great way to keep yourself from carrying your thoughts out into action, although, of course, it depended on the way you thought.

By thinking a certain thought, you could think that you've carried the thought out into action, or done something more.

For a long time I watched, from a spot where the garden of Versailles could be seen at one glance, an autistic looking child flailing his arms in anger, and listened to him screaming his head off, thinking that he was expressing my own state of mind, but at the same time, I felt almost intimidated by the sharp noise and went somewhere else, and picked up a stone from the innermost part of the Versailles Palace, where there was almost no one, and threw it at some birds sitting on a nearby tree, and, having done that, I could finally leave the spot; throwing a ball absentmindedly, or aiming at something, was one of the things that made me feel strangely excited when I was a child, and is still one of my secret hobbies. How many stones had I thrown at rivers and trees as a child?

But the swans of Versailles reminded me of the fact that it wasn't really true that I didn't have anything against swans. I recalled the family of swans, consisting of a couple and two cygnets, that lived in a small pond in a little park in a small French town I once stayed in, where I took regular walks. But one day, the cob literally went crazy, and could no longer control its anger, and did not hide the fact. In the end, it bit both of the cygnets to death, after which it became even more vicious and attacked people, and even after people shut it up in a fence it escaped the fence and continued to attack people, and I was one of the victims.

At the time I chose to flee instead of getting into a ridiculous fight with the swan that suddenly came rushing at me, wounded me slightly by pecking at my buttocks, and again aimed at my weak spot with its huge wings spread out, because it instantly occurred to me that our weapons were much too different—a fight between a swan, which could use nothing but its beak, and me, who could use both my hands and my feet, would be as ludicrous as a fight between a sea lion and a camel—for our fight to be fair. And what I felt after the somewhat awkward incident with the swan, which disappeared from the park soon after—I don't know if it was sent somewhere else or was executed—was a somewhat pleasant sensation, which was also the case when a puppy suddenly appeared from an open gate of someone's house while I was walking in an alley in the town sometime before that, and disappeared back into the gate after lightly biting my leg. Curiously, the puppy had a string with a blue balloon attached to it tied around its neck, and it was possible that the puppy did what it did to me because it was excited or angry over the balloon that a child at that house had hung on it for fun.

And what made it possible for me to leave France, which had made me break up with my girlfriend, were the dragonflies flying in the air over the Versailles Palace. No, perhaps that wasn't true, but I made an effort to think that it was. The dragonflies that flew around in confusion as if they owned the sky drained all my energy, and made me feel strangely uncomfortable, and, above all, dizzy. It seemed that my dizziness wouldn't subside even if I distributed my dizziness all around to the countless dragonflies flying dizzily in the air. I wanted to leave Versailles, and France, in order to get away from the dragonflies, but I couldn't do so right away, for I could get on a flight home only the day after.

And as a result, my ordeal in France continued for a little longer.

I stayed in a cheap Arab hotel at the foot of the Montmartre Hill, the owner of which looked as if he had walked right out of *The Arabian Nights* into reality, being big, with a long beard, and wearing a turban on his head, and looked so indefinably Arab, even when you considered the fact that he was Arab, thus looking like a non-Arab who was disguised as an Arab, but anyway, the inside of the hotel was even shabbier than its shabby exterior.

When night came, I barely managed to fall asleep, being extremely tired and trying to put up with the still-loud noise that came from a nightclub nearby, but soon woke to find, to my surprise, that my body was literally tilted to a side, that the lower part of my body was on the floor, and what was even more surprising was that the bed, too, was tilted along with myself. It was clear that the bed had tilted when one of its legs, temporarily fixed and barely supporting the bed, fell out.

Lying askew on the bed, watching the glittering light of the neon sign of a bar reflected by the window, and listening to the music to which some might be dancing, I thought that I didn't want to have any patience in a place that required great patience, and almost losing my patience, I had the vague thought that by making an issue of everything that could turn into an issue, you could stir up and raise an issue, and at the same time, either find or not find a solution to the issue. The various sounds that came in through the window didn't please me at all, and I thought that I had a good reason for not being pleased. The sounds were actually noises that tormented me, for I had experienced the horrors of noise more than the horrors of anything else, and had never been able to shake off my fear of noise. Several times, I'd felt an intense urge to kill someone all because of noise. One day someone who lived right next door to me played, endlessly and desperately all afternoon, a hymn called "Faith, Hope, and Charity" on a brass wind instrument, either a trumpet or a saxophone, probably practicing for some kind of a church performance, which drove me nearly insane, and I had to, with great effort, keep myself from running over to strangle the person.

But when the noise from the nightclub subsided after a few hours and I tried to sleep again after temporarily fixing the bed leg, there was something else that kept me from falling asleep. Something seemed to be moving very quietly in the silence, and there was, in fact, something moving very quietly. At first, looking at the thing, hovering over the boundary between the circle of the faint light and the shadow created by the bedside lamp, I thought I was dreaming. But the thing, which appeared in the form of a shadow in the beginning, but soon cast off the shadow and revealed itself, gradually came toward me like some kind of a fluid movement being made on the floor, and the thing, which looked like a mouse in every respect, was none other than a mouse, and it was as real as the mirror hanging on a wall and the reflection of a mouse in the mirror. So there was no mouse that appeared before me, and I had not imagined a mouse, listening to the distinct sound made by mice running around busily or cautiously above the ceiling. (I already feel that I've forgotten how and why I've come to tell this story, but that won't really be a problem.)

I considered going down to the counter and waking up the Arab owner, who could be sound asleep, but then I had the feeling that he would, looking dazed as if he had been sleeping for centuries under a spell and had woken up through another spell, tell me to just go back upstairs and quietly try to sleep, with a scolding look on his face, as if mice in the building were nothing to make a fuss about, as if it were only natural that mice lived with men, as if mice, too, had the right to use the room, as if people were surprised or terrified to see mice because they lacked understanding on the order of the world in which they had to coexist with other animals, so I remained where I was.

Looking at the mouse that was looking at me, I tried to think of it as something that was nowhere near a mouse, something that was infinitely far from being a mouse, something that wasn't a mouse, something that wasn't anything at all, and at last came to think of it as such, but at that moment—the mouse continued to stare at me, patting its face with its forepaws, as if trying to make me acknowledge the fact that it was indeed a mouse—I began to think that it was something close to a mouse, and in the end, I came to think once again that it was a mouse, and nothing other than a mouse. So recalling an anecdote about someone who was delighted to see mice on his bed before he died, I thought that this, in a way, was a delightful thing.

Before I knew it the mouse had been joined by two others of its kind. They came closer when I stayed still and stepped back when I stirred or made a sound. As if that were how mice dealt with people. The mice, which had a lot of time on their paws, looked as if they planned to stay up the night with me. It didn't seem like such a bad thing to spend a strange night, staying up with mice. I felt that doing so would require a game we could play together. Depending on the circumstances, I could play around with the mice, or play with them. But although they looked as if they planned to stay up the night with me, they didn't seem to have prepared a game we could play together while staying up the night, and I didn't know what we could do together, either.

Anyway, it occurred to me that with nothing else to eat in the room, there was nothing but my body that the mice could easily choose as their food and be pleased to eat. It was only at that moment I realized that there was a problem between the mice and me that had to be resolved.

I had no particular grudge, hostility, or fear toward the species of animals called mice, and thought that mice, too, were just doing what they were supposed to do in this world into which they had simply had the misfortune of being born as mice, and thought briefly about the persecution and suffering inflicted upon them by men, and the revenge they took on men, and thought that I could give them a part of my body as an offering of sorts, but I couldn't allow that while sitting still, watching a part of my toe being torn off. And at that moment I recalled a story I seemed to have heard from someone. In the story, a man wakes up from sleep to find a mouse sitting on his forehead, about to gnaw on his nose. I wasn't sure if it was a story I had heard from someone, or one that I had imagined myself, but it seemed that something like that might happen if I fell asleep.

I turned off the light again to think calmly and properly about the things I could do with the mice, but I couldn't come up with anything suitable. Nevertheless, I acted as if I wouldn't just sit still, but for some reason, I just sat still. And the mice stayed still, instead of closing the distance between us in the darkness, through which the light from the outside faintly shone, as if they, too, were trying to come up with something suitable. I stared intently at the mice that made me nervous, growing more nervous, while at the same time, making the mice nervous as well.

As I thought about myself and the mice, keeping still in the darkness in somewhat different positions, it occurred to me that the history of the wretched and complete banishment of wild animals, which lost their homes and were driven into literal wilderness, has never been properly dealt with, neither in human history nor animal history, and I felt a kind of guilt about the animals that humans have doggedly driven out. (In this way, I was thinking indirectly about the mice in the darkness which, facing the crisis of banishment, overcame the crisis with wisdom.)

When I turned the light back on in the room, the mice were still in the same spot. It was plain that they hadn't learned to fear men. Or they might have learned to forget to fear. Perhaps they were in the process of evolving from a wild animal into a pet. One of them was primping, again with a gesture characteristic of rodents, sitting balanced on its hind legs and rubbing its face with its somewhat daintily small forepaws. I thought, That's the way mice sit, and the posture they take when they make themselves up, and it's no different from the way women make themselves up. But the mouse wasn't making itself up in that posture to win my approval.

I felt as if the mice were warning me not to fall asleep unguarded, or trying to teach me some sort of humor or sorrow I didn't know, which only they knew, but I just couldn't understand what they were trying to say. So I thought, They don't look like they're carrying daggers, but they could be carrying daggers, only because the expression, carrying daggers, came to my mind while I was looking at the mice. And that made me see just how ridiculous I was in dealing with the mice.

It was a very strange thing to watch a mouse primping in your hotel room in the middle of the night, so I tried to look at it through the eyes of someone looking at it in a strange way, but it wasn't all that strange. (What in the world! There's nothing in this world that's all that strange.) And yet, looking at the strange mice, I thought that they were driving me nearly insane, and before that, thought that I was slowly going insane, which I'd been thinking for a long time, and thought about insanity, and briefly thought about Nietzsche while thinking that perhaps insanity was an ultimate state of being that could be reached by the potential within the self, and wondered what Nietzsche, who probably had a philosophical thought about everything, and must, in my opinion, have had a philosophical thought about green frogs in a pond or screws as well, thought of these animals called mice, and it occurred to me that perhaps Nietzsche felt something unique, different from (or along with) terror or fear, or in other words, what people generally feel about the rodents called mice, but I didn't know what it was that he felt.

I wanted to leave the situation as it was, for it was possible that I may never again have such an experience with mice anywhere. The mice went around the room quite freely now, as if they knew how I felt. It seemed that if I reached out my hand, they would rub themselves against it instead of biting it. In any case, the mice didn't grow more loathsome the more I looked at them or anything. At that moment, however, they began to flee because of the sound of loud footsteps of someone walking down the stairs outside the room. The mice disappeared into a hole somewhere, and did not reappear. They seemed to fear not me, who was in front of them, but someone invisible, someone whose footsteps only they could hear. Or perhaps they didn't really have a good time in my room and went to another room with a hole in it. Only then did I realize that I hadn't made any attempt to chase away the mice, and it seemed that it was I, not the mice, who had wanted to play. But I didn't know how to play with mice, and thought that as a result I'd made the mice waste their precious time. Nevertheless, I felt that the night I spent with the mice in an Arab hotel in Paris, the city of romance, was at least a little fantastic, although it wasn't very romantic.

Having gotten almost no sleep because of the mice, I got up in the end and saw that there was a plate at every corner of the room. A plate of rat poison, no doubt. It was clear that the clever mice hadn't even looked at the poison, so old and stiff that it couldn't possibly appeal to them. It seemed that there should be a notice on the wall for guests, who didn't know anything, that said, Beware not to eat the rat poison, but you may, if you really want to. In the end, I left the hotel at dawn after staying up the night with the mice that the Arab perhaps kept as pets, or that lived in comfort and safety under his care, and could be on my way home.

And now I remember my night with the mice as one of the most memorable experiences I've ever had, and I've come to feel grateful for those mice . . . No, I did feel grateful for them in a way, but the experience wasn't one of the most memorable I've ever had. It was merely one of the many things that were nothing at all.

And having returned home, I thought that if I went to Paris again, I could perhaps run into someone in a park and be invited to his home, and he would take me to a residential boat on the Seine, with an interior like that of an ordinary home, and I could spend the night on the boat, which would rock in the current when other boats passed by. No, that's not true. The day before I spent the night with the mice at the hotel, I actually spent the night on a residential boat floating on the Seine at someone's invitation. The inside of the boat was quite similar to the inside of an ordinary home, and the only thing that indicated that it was a boat was the small, round windows that looked like windows on a boat. But the person who invited me was not the owner of the boat, and he had come to stay on the boat because he met an old woman at the park, and she asked him if he could watch her boat for her, which would be vacant when she went to her summer house. I spent a strange night on a house floating on a river, which wobbled whenever other boats passed by.

I once stayed in a house for several days because the person who was watching it for someone who was on a long trip was going away himself for several days and asked me to watch the house for him, because someone had to take care of the cat there. I had someone else come to my house to take care of the goldfish there. In other words, someone took care of my goldfish, and I took care of someone else's cat. I thought that my goldfish, which lived in a small fishbowl, could go without eating for a few days, or could live on water since it lived in water, but also thought that it would be all right to have someone take care of it for me. I said goodbye to the person going on a trip by telling him to have a good trip, and not to tell me anything about it afterwards.

The cat was somewhat socially inept, and tried to keep as much distance from me as possible. It was very wary of me, and I made it grow even more wary of me by slightly threatening it in a playful way. At the same time, I tried to become better friends with the cat by turning on the television and watching, side by side, programs that I thought cats would like. I mostly turned on programs with cats or mice in them. But although the cat cautiously watched the programs with cats or mice in them, hiding behind the sofa, it never came near me, and perhaps it thought that the cats or the mice, characters in animations, had nothing to do with itself.

Then, seeing on a program a puppy that liked to sing, I tried to get the cat interested, but to no avail. The puppy, which lived in the home of a musician, barked merrily as if singing when it heard the family sing or play an instrument, and curiously, although it didn't react in any way when it heard a pop song, it leapt to its feet when it heard vocal or classical music, even while resting, playing, eating, or even sleeping, and barked in a way that sounded like music.

I once saw on television, while the cat watched me from behind the sofa, the news that someone threatened a taxi driver with a weapon and made him drive somewhere, and then paid him much more than the fare and disappeared. He was a robber, but I wasn't sure if he ended up regretting what he was doing, for some reason, while he was in the act of robbing, or if he had everything planned out from the beginning, from the robbing to the regretting. Did he plan the thing beforehand, and think that by doing so, he could have a pretty good time, and get some sort of a satisfaction from it? Or did he have no choice but to threaten the taxi driver to make him abandon him in a remote and lonely place where taxi drivers were reluctant to go? But to be precise, the cat and I didn't see the news together. I told the cat a story about a serial killer I saw on television another evening. The killer murdered many people, two on a single day once. I tried to imagine what it must feel like to kill two people in a day, but couldn't.

And I took down the family portrait of that someone, which was hanging on the living room wall, a picture that had clearly been taken long ago, and looked, side by side with the cat, at the people in the picture—people who looked like the person's mother and father and younger brother. Also in the picture was a cat that must have died long ago. I fed the cat regularly, even as I tried to think of a way to bring the cat, which avoided me, almost to the point of death without making it quite starve to death. And looking at the cat, I recalled certain facts about cats, such as that they express themselves in mysterious ways, and that in ancient Egypt, where people worshiped cats, people were put to death if they killed a cat, and expressed their sorrow when a cherished cat died by shaving their own eyebrows, and that some cats were clever enough to turn a fan on and off, and I smiled, picturing a cat turning on a fan and enjoying the breeze (animals make us smile so easily, in unexpected ways).

In any case, I felt very comfortable living in someone else's house, taking care of someone's cat in behalf of someone else, so I didn't go outside at all, and for some reason, stayed naked without any clothes on the whole time I was there. Being naked in someone else's house brought me an unusual pleasure, and I felt a little as if I were striding down the street naked, when I was only going from the bedroom to the living room. It was different from being naked in an unfamiliar hotel room.

The house was quite different from my own, in that everything was so well organized. I felt intense displeasure with organized things, and liked to make a mess of the things in my house on purpose, or put them in somewhat unexpected places. I may have developed this habit after getting drunk one night and getting a potato from the kitchen, unaware of what I was doing, and putting it in a drawer in a wardrobe in the living room, which showed how timid I was, never getting out of control even when I was drunk, and finding the potato in the drawer several days later, which made me feel as happy as if I had found a relic. Next to the bottles of sleeping pills in my kitchen cabinet there are Bolivian milk someone gave me as a present, a bottle of salt I brought from a desert, and again, bottles of salt and other seasonings and pepper shakers, and a little stuffed salamander which was also a present from someone. And under my bed there are several shoe boxes, some of which contain dried up flowers with long stalks, including poppies, and some of which contain pictures I took while traveling, although I don't normally like taking pictures, of chairs and benches I sat or lay down on, and of myself reflected in a mirror in a hotel room I stayed in, feeling somewhat awkward in the room I was staying in for the first time, and strangely, my eyes looked fierce in the pictures. In a little room in my house you couldn't really call a library, full of messy piles of books, as well as suitcases and other odds and ends, there's an organ that someone threw away in an alley, which I brought home. The organ is missing a few keys and a pedal, but it still sounds like an organ. I've never learned how to play the piano or the organ but can read music a little, so from time to time, I'd go into the little room and play Bach's Toccata and Fugue, pressing the keys very slowly with one hand, and I thought repeatedly that the music suited death, and also thought that the performance was solely for the things in that room, such as the chairs and drawers.

Anyway, what I took care of mostly, in the house I went to in order to take care of a cat, was a plant in that house. It was a sweet oleander, poisonous from the leaves to the roots, and its white sap, in particular, could kill you if it so much as touched your bruised skin. I say I took care of it, but all I did was water it once, and what I did mostly was think about the poison that filled up the body of the plant.

I spent a lot of time thinking random thoughts, sitting naked, motionless like a chameleon, in a wooden chair that was at a corner of the living room of someone else's empty house, which I left my own house to stay in, and among the thoughts were the memory of looking at the Eiffel Tower, a part of which could be seen through the window, and the wallpaper in the room, in a hotel in Paris, and the memory of the sound of a kitten crying, which I heard in my house once, and the memory of being inde-scribably touched as a child when I fell asleep one day in the middle of the day, listening to the sound of countless silkworms quietly munching on mulberry leaves in a corner of the room, and then woke up to see them squirming quietly. The sound of silkworms munching on mulberry leaves was a sound that was at the heart of the kind of peace I experienced only in my childhood, a sound that wasn't quite a noise, although it was a noise, and sounded infinitely pleasant for that reason, and it brought me great pleasure. It suddenly occurred to me that there may never have been a moment in my life when I was genuinely happy, except for the moments when I was happy for no reason at all, and for that reason, I was sad for a moment.

And I also thought for a moment about the person who was taking care of my goldfish for me at my house, and about the time when I watched the goldfish for several hours wanting to learn something about its everyday life. And I thought about a woman I used to know. She had a six-year-old nephew at the time, and although he was very young, he was so wicked as to lead you to reflect deeply on evil, on human nature. It was nothing unusual for him to hit other children, and he touched women's bodies without feeling any shame at all—he mostly tried to get his hands into women's skirts one way or another, and not being content with that, tried to get himself into women's skirts—and went around cursing all the time. No one was able to figure out what extraordinary phenomenon took place in the child's mind to turn him into such a fiend. It was nearly impossible to change his nature, and he ended up in a juvenile delinquent facility when he got older. When he was little, when people asked him what he wanted to be when he grew up, he always said that he wanted to be a soldier in the national armed forces, which was distinctly different from a child saying that he wanted to be a soldier when he grew up.

And I recalled something the woman told me, how when a

military coup broke out in the city she lived in as a child and citizens were slaughtered, the first victim in the city was probably a cat, not a person, although she wasn't sure if she had dreamt it or imagined it (I realized at that moment that the reason why I thought, in mist-shrouded Venice, that the first victim of some wars or revolutions was a cat or some other animal was because of what she told me). Perhaps that was true. Perhaps the soldiers of the armed forces deployed to suppress the protesters had no experience killing, and shot to death an animal, a cat, before they committed their first murder, whereby they gained confidence and carried out genocide. During the French Revolution, in fact, it was a sheep, not a man, that became the first to die at the guillotine. So people used a sheep to test the performance of the newly invented guillotine. Anyway, she thought that an anecdote about the sacrifice of a cat should be included in the history of the well-known massacre.

What I spent the most time thinking about while thinking about her, however, was someone she knew. A friend of hers went on a trip with several people, said he was stepping out for a moment while having a meal at a seaside restaurant, and left, never to return. With that, he disappeared without a trace. No one knew if he was abducted or disappeared on his own. She believed that he must have committed suicide by jumping into the sea. People who committed suicide could show different behavior from usual just before committing suicide, but it was quite possible for them to act no different from usual.

And recalling how I once spent time making a list of things that were neither good nor bad for passing the time, I tried to recall the list, but nothing came to mind other than that I played my own requiem with a few notes on the broken organ. When evening finally came, I took out a handful of wilted lettuce from the fridge and quietly chewed on it, and the first thing I knew, I was chewing, without realizing it, the way a goat chews grass. And eating a banana after finishing the lettuce, as if having dessert, I felt as if I were a goat, as well as a monkey, a hairless ape. I realized that in order to suddenly realize that you were distant relatives with monkeys, it was enough to sit naked, imitating a monkey, scratching yourself without thinking, or eating a banana.

And I thought that the reason why I thought a lot about other animals was because a general lack of interest in human things led me to descend and ascend into an animal world, and into a transcendental world. And there seemed to be a world somewhere between the descent and the ascent where you couldn't stay, but could at least go in and out of.

And the next day while quietly eating an apricot I'd brought with me, I recalled how I gave apricots to a cow I encountered on a country road in France, and thought about a man who stayed home alone doing nothing for a period of time in his youth, then suddenly became a bulldozer driver one day and drove bulldozers for several years, and then went on an ocean ship for several years, after which he returned home and spent several years doing nothing—or did he go on an ocean ship for several years in his youth, then return home and do nothing for several years, and then one day suddenly become a bulldozer driver and drive bulldozers for several months, and again spend a period of time staying home alone doing nothing?—and was found dead, sitting on a chair in a corner of his living room.

The story about the man, which I wasn't sure was true or not, was something I heard from an anesthesiologist. When I thought about the man, I always pictured him with his back turned to the world, or, rather, with the world's back turned to him, and imagined that he drove a bulldozer and got on an ocean ship with the lethargy of his lone years in which he did nothing. For at times, lethargy becomes the greatest source of strength. Could it be that perhaps a strength that was the complete opposite of passion had provoked the greatest passion in him?

I also recalled how the anesthesiologist said that he had signed contracts with several hospitals, and mostly anesthetized patients requiring a big surgery, after which he would spend up to ten hours, until the anesthesia wore off, waiting somewhere near the patient, reading a novel or fantasizing, and how he said he wanted to turn the story about the dead man into a novel. His life didn't seem all that different from that of the man he told me about. And although I don't know if it was true or not, he said that sometimes he put himself under anesthesia and indulged in the pleasure of the hallucination that came over him as he was being anesthetized.

The story about the life of the man, who spent most of his time in loneliness despite driving a bulldozer and getting on an ocean ship, had a strange hold on my heart, not because his life was dramatic, but because I could sense a certain majestic loneliness in him.

And I thought of someone I saw on television who lived a life similar to that of the ocean ship sailor, gathering huge mushrooms growing on trees in a birch forest in Alaska, and someone else who lived in Greenland, catching birds with a little net. These people, immigrants who left their homelands long ago, lived like people with some big secrets—but it was possible that they didn't have any secrets—like people who cultivated some big secrets. In any case, they seemed to me to be enjoying some kind of a secret pleasure, and in a way seemed to take after Wittgenstein. (At the time, I was very slowly reading a book on Wittgenstein, which was as difficult to understand as books written by Wittgenstein.)

I imagined creating a self-contained world of my own in which communication was impossible and unnecessary. Perhaps the very thing that constitutes a person's inherent nature is something that can't be understood by others. Only the thoughts that I couldn't share in their entirety with another person seemed to be my genuine thoughts. I thought that the emphasis on communication, rampant among people and even forced upon them, was so excessive that, in a way, it kept a man from squarely facing the fact that he was, in the end, alone—how right are the words of Nietzsche, who said that a man merely experiences his own self, that he experiences a world distorted by his own self?—and made severance and isolation, things that were actually necessary, seem undesirable, and thought about how unstable and imperfect communication itself was, whose possibility may be nothing more than an illusion, and thought that you could go down deeper and withdraw into yourself, finding peace there, and that perhaps Wittgenstein, too, who stayed withdrawn deep in his own world, working as an assistant gardener, was able to communicate with the world on a different level, through the isolation he brought on himself.

Wittgenstein, who studied mechanical engineering and mathematics, then logic and philosophy and music, and fought in the First World War, and wrote, while at prison camp, *Tractatus Logico-Philosophicus*, which later became widely known, and also worked as an assistant gardener at a monastery where he lived as a recluse, probably spent a period of his life quietly bending and unbending his body in the silence of the monastery, cutting branches from trees, gathering fallen leaves, and fertilizing trees.

I imagined that perhaps it was while he was gardening or when he woke up from a brief nap while working in the garden—at which moment he may have recalled the war he had fought in, during which he may have escaped several deaths, and reflected on how far he had come from the war, and at the same time, how close the war was in his memory—that Wittgenstein, who fought in the last war in which romantic elements still loomed in the air despite the smoke of gunpowder and the smell of blood, a war in which horses were still used as an important mode of transportation, and soldiers in confrontation shared the food they made with each other, and people may have begun a new day's fight by asking how each other's night was, and whose two nephews fought each other as enemies in the next world war, came up with his important ideas.

It's pleasant to think that Wittgenstein, two of whose older brothers committed suicide and one either committed suicide or disappeared, and who acquired a patent by doing a research that led to the development of the helicopter about thirty years later, and went to a small town in Norway in order to study logic without any disturbance, and studied the problem of color and the problem of certainty, and died two days after writing the last part of his book, *On Certainty,* and then, losing consciousness, thought about the air mechanics and parts of a helicopter while doing garden work, such as cutting tree branches and sweeping dead leaves, although I don't know if he did so in reality.

When I was lost in my own thoughts, the cat that kept me at a distance would come near me, but when I tried to come near it, it would withdraw, and I would inflict several forms of torture, which were possible only in thought, upon the cat that was hiding somewhere or passing quietly in front of me, and picturing the cat in agony and passing out in the end, I would say something that was appropriate for saying to a cat in such a state, for instance, What we can say to a cat incessantly scratching its face is that wherever we go, we float down with empty chairs, surrounded by words.

And I named the cat, which had a name given by its owner, Maoist, although I didn't call it by the name. I named it Maoist because one day while I was with the cat, I saw on television the news that Maoists had come into power in Nepal. I watched the news with Maoist the cat, which knew nothing at all about communism, which, without any grounds, made the cat seem like a true communist to me.

And thinking about Maoists' Nepal, I tried to become better friends with the cat I named Maoist, but we never grew closer than when we first met. Maoist the cat, which had no thoughts of its own, looked like a Maoist when it was wandering around the house or sitting quietly somewhere, but when it was pooping in its sand-filled toilet, it seemed to go back to being an ordinary cat. Nevertheless, I told Maoist the cat about a cat named Tango that I saw on television one day, that left home and somehow appeared in the back of the stage for a British talk show that was being broadcast live, but I' didn't tell the cat about the fact that Mao Zedong mostly rode a rickshaw during the Long March, which was 9,000 kilometers long, or the fact that Yasser Arafat, the Palestinian leader, spent a lot of time raptly watching the cartoon "Tom and Jerry," although he didn't read a single book in the forty years before he died (I suddenly wondered which character Arafat identified with, and which he sided with as he watched "Tom and Jerry," and if he didn't come up with a strategy that would be helpful in fighting those he saw as his enemies while watching the cartoon, but I had no way of finding out). And I wondered whether or not it was right to tell Maoist the cat that in a certain area of the world at a certain period of time, there was a custom of burying cats alive in a wall in the house, but in the end, I did.

One day, Maoist the cat was walking on the keys of the piano whose lid I kept open, and it went carefully back and forth several times on the keys, even though it was quite startled and a little frightened by the sound that came when the keys were pressed, as if the sound raised its curiosity and brought it some kind of a pleasure, and did so several more times after that. I came to enjoy listening to the music played by Maoist the cat, a musician now, and I gave titles to the music it performed ad lib, differently each time, such as "Blue Rapture," "Crumbling Sorrow," or "Uncontrollable Dizziness."

And as I watched the cat, the cat I had long ago came to my mind. The cat, which I named Ramsay—was it because there was a genius mathematician by a similar name, or was it because of the name of the characters in *To the Lighthouse*?—loved it when I picked it up and threw it very high, and sometimes I threw it so high inside the house that it hit the ceiling with its head, but the cat loved it, as if it enjoyed being dizzy from hitting its head.

And sitting in a chair feeling dizzy, I thought about my dizziness, and thought that dizziness, like boredom, could be a condition of existence. And for the first time, I thought that perhaps I could examine the cause for my dizziness, and that the reason why I had never thought that there could be a cause for my dizziness, that I could find out the cause, was because the dizziness, which became obvious with my swooning, came to me so naturally, and so secretly at first, and became a natural part of me.

In the end, I spent several days with the cat that kept me at a distance, doing almost nothing, and returned home after getting several mosquito bites. The person who returned from his trip gave me a little wooden carving of a reclining Buddha as a gift, because I told him that I went to an antique shop in Nepal once, and saw a little wooden horse there and liked it so much that I wanted to buy it, but gave up because it was actually too big, and bought a sitting Buddha statue that was next to the horse, after which I began collecting Buddha statues. It was true that I bought a sitting Buddha statue in Nepal, but I was joking when I said that I was collecting Buddha statues. The reclining Buddha looked shoddy even at a glance and looked shoddier the more you looked at it, and made you question the sincerity of the giver, so thinking about him, I thought that it would've been better for him to not give me anything at all, but shortly put a stop to the thought. But I kept thinking about him, who was a good person but had a very stupid side to him, which is what made it difficult for me to deal with him, and so I thought that I shouldn't deal with him anymore. But I was wrong. He was a good person, and not stupid. So I thought that perhaps he had a reason for giving me such a shoddy gift. When I did, the reclining Buddha looked like some kind of a riddle.

Before I left Nepal I went to an antique shop and bought a somewhat shoddy wooden carving of a sitting Buddha on whose lap sat a woman, her legs spread out, which looked blasphemous and sensuous at the same time. I wrapped toilet paper around its upper body and put it under the bed at first and then under the desk, and I continue to put it here and there, not having found the right spot for it yet.

But now I had two statues of Buddha, and could start a collection of Buddha statues. It also occurred to me that perhaps I could, with great difficulty, carve the solid statue and make a statue of a cat or Maria. I could turn it into a cat or Maria that came out of Buddha, or into something that wasn't anything at all.

The man, who was darkly tanned, told me, who hadn't asked him anything about his trip, about the time he explored the jungle one afternoon. You couldn't really say that he explored, for what he did was follow a relatively well maintained forest path with a guide showing the way. He said that he fell behind, suddenly tired of being led as a group by a tour guide like children on a school excursion, and entered the jungle, imagining that while following the path into the jungle, he might arrive at a community of natives who lived almost in the nude, and be invited to the home of a kind native and have roasted iguana or lizard for dinner, and then about midway through crossing an old rope bridge that looked quite dangerous, he suddenly ran into a huge coiled up snake that looked splendid and beautiful—the rope bridge was so narrow that you couldn't pass through unless the other party stepped aside—and without realizing what he was doing, he took out the fan he had and opened it up, and when the snake, quite startled for some reason—considering that snakes don't have good eyesight, it was more likely that the snake was startled by the sound of the fan that suddenly opened up, than by the sight of the fan that suddenly opened up—fell into the water under the bridge—the bridge wasn't high, and the snake didn't seem in danger of losing its life, having fallen on water, and although the snake got quite a scare, it was fine—he felt almost happy that he was there, he said.

Afterwards I for some reason wrapped bandage all over the reclining Buddha, whose giver seemed to have posed a riddle for me, and which itself seemed like a riddle, because I thought about wrapping a scarf around the reclining Buddha's neck while picturing the black girl I saw in a subway station in Coney Island, unwrapping the scarf around her neck, but then thought that bandage might be better than a scarf. But it suddenly occurred to me that I forgot to rub Vaseline on the reclining Buddha, because I once thought about the pleasant feeling that comes when pronouncing the word Vaseline, a compound word of the words water and oil, the name of a petroleum extract used as a healing ointment for the injured during the first and second world wars, and used for too many purposes at one time, while picturing a pantomime with no action or sound, in which a Buddha with

Vaseline rubbed all over the body, a Vaseline Buddha, you could call it, quietly sits in a little room whose floor, ceiling, and four walls are covered in Vaseline, a room gushing Vaseline and gradually becoming filled with it. And I thought that I could give the title *Vaseline Buddha*—the name was something that could be given to something indefinable, something unnamable, and also meant untitled—to what I was writing, but as soon as I did, I thought that it wasn't a good idea, and as soon as I thought that perhaps this story had its beginning when I sat cross-legged in the middle of my room one day, thinking of Vaseline Buddha, and picturing the Buddha buried and melting in Vaseline, I thought that it wasn't really true, and after thinking that when I unwrapped the bandage, I should perhaps hold a mirror up to the reclining Buddha, I put it under my bed, reclining, and from time to time, I lowered my head and looked at the Buddha, reclining peacefully under the bed, and recited at random, to pass the time, Buddhist mantras, such as om mani padme hum, maha prajna paramita, and doro amitabha. And I thought that a name like Fasting Clown could suit the bandaged Buddha, but that I could give him the name, The Difficulty of Light Swimming on Difficult Waters, or The Difficulty of a Water Strider Walking on Difficult Waters, because someone who performed the miracle of walking on water came to my mind, and I thought that perhaps he got the idea of performing the miracle from a water strider.

But when I returned home a dead goldfish was waiting for me. The person who watched my house for me while I was away didn't say anything about the death of the fish. At night, I put the goldfish in a plastic bag and went to a cemetery by the river, where I took a walk now and then. Once, looking out at the sea, I thought that the sea was a huge grave for fish—I pictured the countless dead fish in the sea, and the sea was the biggest grave in the world—so I thought that I should bury the goldfish in the pond where it once lived, but I couldn't think of a suitable pond.

The cemetery was a burial ground for missionaries who were beheaded while proselytizing Christianity during a period in the past. I dug up a bit of the soil in front of a missionary's grave and buried the goldfish. The place, where beheaded missionaries were buried, and which overlooked a river, seemed the perfect grave for a fish, and I felt that by burying it there, I gave the fish a proper funeral. I suddenly recalled that the Danish word kierkegaard means churchyard, and I named the dead fish Kierkegaard, which seemed to suit the fish. And I was pleased by the fact that I was the only one who knew that a fish named Kierkegaard lay sleeping in a graveyard for missionaries, and that I could come to a kierkegaard, or a churchyard, whenever I wished and think about Kierkegaard the fish and Kierkegaard the philosopher.

Anyway, there were moments when I felt so dizzy that I really felt as if I would die, and wanted desperately to die for that reason. Or could I say I wanted desperately to die, and felt as if I would die for that reason? At any rate, I learned that a desire to die could be more desperate than a desire for anything else. My consciousness was urging me, badgering me to come to a decision, but I didn't listen, not even to my own consciousness

I still thought about suicide only in a faint, vague way, and in fact, I've never thought properly about it. And my idea of suicide in those days was a quite playful one, regarding the issue of whether a person who committed suicide behaved no differently from usual, or differently from usual.

Still, I had a lethal dose of sleeping pills, which I could use whenever I wished, a part of which I kept in a music box I bought as a souvenir on a trip. From time to time, I opened the music box to check up on the sleeping pills, and when I looked at them, listening to the music box, they always raised some kind of a hope in me, and put me at ease. Perhaps I could take the sleeping pills and wind the spring, and fall into eternal sleep while listening to the music box play.

I didn't see phantoms, but I saw signs, visions, that foretold the coming of phantoms before long. Once, in the middle of the night, I suddenly woke up in bed and saw a large black dog quietly sitting in the darkness of the room, and took it into my sleep and let it lead me to a mysterious place, and before I knew it, we were surrounded by a countless number of other large black dogs. Seeing the vision, I thought about having a chat with phantoms when they actually came.

And what enabled me to just barely endure the depression that seemed as if it would lead to death were the thoughts I had in secret. Thinking those thoughts, I smiled to myself at times. And the smile I smiled to myself in secret, while rereading *Molloy* for the first time in a long time, during days when there was almost nothing to smile about, seemed my only genuine smile, and the smile, which wasn't different from a certain kind of sneer, was directed at strange things. But at times, all kinds of smile, not just that smile, seemed strange, and awful as well.

I applied modifiers, such as corrosive, or sparkling, or coagulative, to my smile, and thought that I could apply them to my dizziness as well. In any case, such modifiers endowed a smile and dizziness with physical characteristics, and I felt that my smile and dizziness were physical states.

But from some time on, I no longer smiled even that smile, and I felt as if I were an empty house where no sound was heard anymore, abandoned by the people who had once lived there, talking and laughing. I also had the vague thought that perhaps my smile, which had vanished like an erased figure in an ancient wall painting, could be found only in the expression of a character in a novel I hadn't yet written.

And the thought led to some thoughts on smile or laughter itself. The ability to smile or laugh is probably one of the things that distinguish humans from other animals. I don't know if other animals smile or laugh, but it doesn't seem that they burst out laughing as humans do, or quietly smile to themselves. It seems that animals only make a pleased sound or wag their tails in contentment. But humans smile or laugh when they're having an interesting experience, when they're in an awkward situation in which they don't know what to do, and even over nothing at all. And sometimes, they laugh until their stomachs hurt, or chuckle, or smile reluctantly, about trivial things, or at other times about something huge, or even as they're trembling with anger over life. Smile or laughter is something that's the closest to, or depending on circumstances, the furthest away from, humans. Smile or laughter, which is so familiar to humans, is actually not as simple as it seems, and difficult to understand. For example, let's take a look at some different kinds and aspects of smile and laughter. They are countless, including a hearty laughter, a wry smile, a sneer, a smile of satisfaction, a dumbfounded smile, a foolish smile, a grin, a loud laughter, a giggle, a quiet smile, a groveling smile, a cunning smile, a smile you put on when you look down on someone or when you're not pleased with someone, just before you're stripped of a smile, a nasty smile, a big smile that spreads across your face, a big nasty smile that spreads across your face, and so on. And then there's a crooked smile. I'm not sure what a crooked smile is exactly, but my smiles always have the feel of one.

There's no other expression of human emotion that has as many qualities and aspects to it as does smile or laughter, which can be preceded by many descriptive words. Laughter can easily arise in inappropriate situations, and in fact, it often arises from the discrepancy between a person and the situation he's faced with. Smile or laughter itself, of course, doesn't function as a full emotion, nor is it something that can be categorized as an emotion, but it reveals the complexities of the heart, being linked to various emotions, and establishes the workings of the mind, interacting with the senses. In addition, smile or laughter, which is the most complex emotional reaction, exerts a powerful influence on emotion and thought. For instance, a person can smile or laugh while deep in sorrow, or when his anxiety reaches its height, and such smile or laughter can change or dispel the sorrow or anxiety. Smile or laughter is the most innocent yet cunning at the same time, the most frivolous yet just as profound, and the most naïve, yet evil. But it's difficult to contemplate evil sorrow, frivolous emptiness, or cunning solitude. The smile or laughter of a newborn baby is probably the most innocent and beautiful thing in the world, but the smile or laughter of someone taking pleasure in abusing someone is evil beyond measure. Perhaps the reason why smile or laughter can so easily change in nature is because unlike emptiness or boredom or such, in which state you can't help but stay for a while once you're in it, smile or laughter is a state in which it's difficult to stay, because smile or laughter is something so unpredictable that it can betray itself. Smile or laughter, which is actually a subtle and complex movement of facial muscles and the mind, is an anthropological object of study as well as a psychological phenomenon (I vaguely imagine that the decisive factor in the human evolution from apes was the human smile or laughter, and humans' awareness of their own smile or laughter). In addition, smile or laughter is a philosophical topic, and many philosophers, in fact, considered smile or laughter from a philosophical point of view.

But one of the problems surrounding laughter is that today, there's an excess and abuse thereof. Laughter, in fact, has become a sublime virtue as well as a sublime vice of the day. Laughter, of course, didn't become such on its own. People seem to be suffering from an obsession to laugh, and steeped in the wrong belief that they can forget past hurts and present sufferings and move forward only by doing so. Fundamental human emotions, such as a sense of emptiness, boredom, loneliness, anxiety, sadness, and unease have become something negative that should be avoided as much as possible, and laughter rules in splendor in the place from which they have been cast out (I picture laughter looking down on the sadness of the emotions it has driven out, without even hiding its nastiness, which, in a way, seems to be the self-portrait of the day). In short, the idea that laughter is desirable, no matter what, is prevalent, like a superstition. But is it true that laughter is just desirable? It's true that laughter has a great power that makes it possible to endure a difficult life, brings the hope that you can break away from an oppressive condition, purifies the mind the way profound sorrow does, assimilates you with the object of laughter, just as when you experience something beautiful, and that the more painful the present situation is, the more necessary is laughter. But the negative effects of laughter are just as serious as the positive. Laughter, by its inherent nature, can cunningly make an individual turn his eyes away from his life and the situation with which he's faced, and make him think less or give up on thinking, thus making him stupid. What good is it to laugh in a futile, unnatural way in the face of a reality that won't change much at all through a little laughter? You could be even more miserable when you face your real self after laughing in vain. In a way, laughter exercises an oppressive ideological function in this era, just as an oppressive system did. I think that the laughter forced upon you by the many soap operas, shows, and movies that you couldn't possibly watch if you had any refinement at all, that drain you of all energy if you watch them, is putting everyone in a state of insensibility and numbness. What those shows, which tell you to laugh in whatever way you can, to laugh until you're in a daze, but aren't funny and only make you sad and furious, really propagate is that you should laugh a lot, for that will keep you from thinking, and your troubles will be covered up by laughter, and won't exist when covered up, and even if they still exist, you're happy as long as you're laughing. (There's nothing more grotesque than a group of people having dinner, laughing as they watch a vulgar comedy program on television.) Genuine laughter always has its beginning in proper humor, and is not separate from the intellect and the reflective power of the intellect. Genuine laughter has enduring strength, but vulgar laughter is strongly volatile, and lacks humor. Sadly, laughter arising from humor, founded in good sense and requiring a natural process, is growing increasingly scarce.

Reflecting thus, I laughed bitterly. And laughter, though weak, found me again before long, but it seemed like the laughter of an idiot I met on the street, a stranger, directed at me.

I continued to be in a poor condition in many ways, but I hadn't yet reached a state in which the poor condition had continued for so long that I didn't care, but I wasn't in a state in which I could do something in a new, bad mood, either.

Anyway, what kept my poor condition from growing worse, no, kept me, to an extent, from completely crumbling, was my son. Or I should say that the thought crossed my mind. But I wasn't sure if that was really the case. I kind of thought that my son wasn't able to keep me from growing worse by thinking worse thoughts. I didn't have the kind of relationship that most fathers have with their children with my son.

My son didn't live with me, and when vacation started, I brought him home and we spent several days together. I tried to spend as much time with him as possible, but it wasn't easy for me to spend time with him.

My son, who, as most children do, let me down, by being born as a boy even though I wanted a girl, and let me down again by looking like a girl at first but growing more and more into a boy, seemed bright but somewhat slow in a way, and as for myself, I tried not to be someone he didn't need, at least, or was better off without.

Once I taught him how to catch rabbits using a wire snare, not because I thought it was something that all the fathers in the world should teach their sons in all ages, but because we didn't really have anything to do together when we actually met, and I happened to think of snares. We lay a snare on a path that no one used, on a mountain at the back of my house where no rabbits lived, and when we returned later, there was nothing in the snare, of course, let alone a rabbit.

And once I bought him a slingshot. It seems incredible now, but as a boy, I made slingshots out of branches and rubber bands and caught birds with them, and I thought about making him a slingshot myself, but didn't want to bother. (I don't know about anything else, but I just can't bring myself to do bothersome things, and although I did unpleasant things even while thinking I didn't want to, I couldn't do the same with bothersome things. So when there's something that I must do, I do it thinking, if possible, that it's something unpleasant rather than bothersome.)

With the slingshot we went to the mountain to catch a magpie, since there were only magpies there. I demonstrated how to use the slingshot, but that didn't go so well, either. (It seemed that there was an eccentric old man in me, as old as could be and willing to lose all his judgment, as well as a boy around ten years of age wanting to remain in the peace of childhood, and the two appeared alternately, and the problem arose when the old man and the boy, who usually got along pretty well, looked down on each other, and a bigger problem arose when the old man and the boy faded away, and an awkward adult who found everything bothersome appeared, and that was the case when I was dealing with my boy.) Nevertheless, he practiced how to use the slingshot as I taught him, but he wasn't very good at it, just as expected. And yet, after we climbed a steep hill, both gasping for breath because my liver was damaged from smoking, which I couldn't quit, and his wasn't fully developed yet, something amazing happened, and a stone he threw casually at a magpie sitting on a branch, which missed the target, hit the wing of a magpie that was flying up into the air, which wobbled for a moment, then steadied itself and flew away, and seeing that, he got excited and jumped up and down for joy. Seeing his great delight, I thought that it wasn't something to get so excited about that you had to jump up and down for joy. Still, I told him something that wasn't far off, that with a slingshot, you could make something like a roe deer, which lives in bigger mountains, black out for a moment although you couldn't kill it, and my son, who already has a problem believing most of what I say even though he's only nine, said with a twinkle in his eyes that we should go to a bigger mountain right away and catch something bigger, and I told him that I knew how he felt, but he should wait a little longer, until he was a little bigger.

Nevertheless, I instructed him to practice more so that he could shoot a flying magpie for real, and feeling triumphant, he practiced till the sun went down, not to do as I instructed but, it seemed, to shoot a flying magpie for real. But he didn't practice for that long, because the sun soon went down. He could have kept practicing after dark, but he gave up. He took after me and lacked perseverance.

I thought that I wasn't sure what I could do for him, but that I wasn't sure, either, if I could do anything and everything if it were for him, and regardless of that thought, I thought of things I should teach him as a father, and taught him how to swim. For some reason, I thought that I had to make sure to teach him how to float on water, how not sink when you fell in water. But he gave up soon after swallowing a few gulps of water, and was reluctant to do anything that involved the possibility of having to swallow water. So I taught him how to jump ropes and do sit-ups, which didn't involve drinking water, and although he couldn't jump the rope even once, he could do sit-ups quite well, as if he'd been doing it for a long time, ever since he was born, even though it was his first time, and did thirty sit-ups at once the night I taught him, possessed with a strange enthusiasm, as if he took great pleasure in it, and didn't listen to me when I told him to stop, and did thirty more, and in the end, reached a hundred, sounding out of breath—he made me kneel down and hold his ankles, and count to a hundred, and I thought about stopping him but I stopped myself from stopping him and watched as he, too, counted the numbers, folding his body in half and unfolding it, and gasping for breath, and as I did I felt something like the sorrow of a father who has a son, not too severely, but mildly, no, severely and mildly at the same time—and at last fell asleep, utterly exhausted, which seems appropriate only for a child, but is somewhat strange even for a child.

And once I taught him how to spin a top, but he didn't have an easy time learning it, and we were both beset with great difficulty until he could spin a top properly. But once he learned how to spin a top he became hooked, and buried himself in spinning a top both at home and outside. As a result, I had to feel a dizziness that was different from my usual dizziness, watching the top he was spinning, which spun around in a circle that was a vivid black and red and blue, so I tried, much too hard, to focus on the red at the center so that the other two colors next to it would disappear and no longer be seen, which made the dizziness grow worse.

There really was quite a strange side to him, which I confirmed one day when I finally woke up around four in the afternoon because I'd drunk too much the night before to find him sitting quietly on the edge of the bed with his back to me. He sat by himself without waking me up till that hour, only drinking water like someone fasting, and at that moment he seemed not just strange, but a little scary as well. Next to me, on the bed, there was some kind of a castle he'd built with Lego blocks. He never told me if he hadn't completed it or if he'd torn it down after completing it because I never asked him about it. That day, I had the ridiculous idea that perhaps I could take him, or make him take me on a journey, and start a true life of wandering as Molloy did, not just go on a trip.

I asked him what he was thinking, and he, with a look of severe reproof on his face, told me that he couldn't tell me that, and so I was able to conclude that he was once again thinking negative thoughts about me. It seemed to me that he was thinking about ordering me around and making me do something when I woke up, condemning me in his young heart.

Fortunately, his anger soon subsided when I bought him a pinwheel. For some reason I wanted to see the pinwheel, which spun quickly when he ran toward me, holding it in his hand, spin more quickly and frantically, so I told him to run faster, and watching him run frantically toward me several times, I thought that we could be good friends someday. But a thought I'd had earlier, that taking after me, he might follow in my ways, came to my mind again and worried me, but I concluded that he would live a life of his own. And when he grew older and life felt unbearable, he would blame me at times, but there was still time before that happened, and it wasn't something inevitable, so it was possible that things wouldn't turn out that way. I had trouble falling asleep that night, watching my son sleeping, and thinking about the first romantic relationship and sexual intercourse he would experience, and the many dreams he would have and then give up, and thinking that for now, he could just keep up with doing what he wanted to do, doing sit-ups, for instance.

Sometimes when we went to the mountain together, he would run around playing, but then sit down on a tree stump and become quietly lost in thought, and when I saw him sitting like that, I would recall my own childhood, when I spent countless hours quietly sitting like that.

It's midwinter now. I'm sitting in the afternoon sun, drinking tea, in front of the table by the window on the second floor of the house I live in. The tea is ginger. The doctor told me that it would help with my dizziness. I do some things as the doctor instructs, but not others. The doctor has banned me from caffeine, but it seems boring somehow to do everything as the doctor ordered, so sometimes, I wake up in the morning and have three cups of strong coffee, and when I do, I grow severely dizzy. But being in that state brings me a strange pleasure. I've now come to think that there's something in my dizziness that has to do with something fundamental in my being, and that dizziness may be something at the root of existence. And dizziness is addictive. It seems that there's something of a religious experience in losing consciousness when dizziness reaches its extreme, or saturation, or freezing point of sorts, which is demonstrated in cases in which people lose consciousness with the help of charms or medicines in certain religious ceremonies. (Sometimes, people make a deliberate attempt to lose consciousness. People on an island in a tropical region dry up the roots of a plant of the pepper family called kava and mix it with water and drink it before performing a ceremony, and then walk on hot stones, and it is said that the drink makes you hallucinate a little and grow averse to light, and that the origin of the ceremony of walking on stones while your senses are paralyzed has to do with eels.)

In the meantime, I ended up going to an ear, nose, and throat clinic. The third floor office of the clinic specializing in symptoms of dizziness was full of people suffering from symptoms of dizziness. Some of them were sitting with their head against the back of the sofa, or leaning on the person next to them, who had come as their guardian. I wanted to put my head on someone's shoulder, and felt a sense of fellowship with them, but I couldn't tell if they felt the same way (perhaps people suffering from the same illness feel a stronger sense of fellowship than that felt among any others).

An old man sitting to my right said to a young man sitting to my left, skipping over me, as if I weren't sitting between them—they didn't know each other—that he'd passed out a few days earlier and passed out twice the day before he came to the clinic, and he sounded as if he were bragging in a way, and I didn't dare say a word in front of him about my own swooning.

I was able to see the doctor at last after waiting for over an hour. He asked me specifically how I was dizzy, but I had difficulty describing my dizziness specifically, so I wanted to tell him that it felt similar to an LSD trip but didn't. I'd never experienced an LSD trip, and knew only through a book that there was something similar between LSD trips and my dizziness. The treatment involved making me dizzy through artificial means to find out the cause of the symptoms of dizziness. I had to put up with the ridiculous tests the doctor conducted on me, the process of which seemed so inadequate that I wondered if the cause could be determined through the tests.

After the checkup, the doctor showed me an anatomical chart of the ear, and told me that there was something wrong with the blood vessel connecting the vestibular organ in one of my ears to the brain, and I thought about my blood vessel that wasn't functioning properly. And I looked at the three semicircular canals and the cochlea connected to the vestibular organ in the anatomical chart. I looked at them with great curiosity, as I always do when I see body organs in an anatomical chart, and they looked amazing and beautiful, like complex mechanisms. The doctor told me that unlike other organs in the body that were connected to each other through many blood vessels, which propelled other blood vessels into action when one of the blood vessels stopped functioning properly, there was only one blood vessel there, and that a surgery was almost impossible, and I realized that I would be living with some kind of a chronic disease, and felt that another problem had been added to the chronic problems I had.

After prescribing some medicine, the doctor banned me from cigarettes, alcohol, and coffee. All three were very difficult things for me to give up. And he taught me several physical movements that would be helpful in overcoming symptoms of dizziness. Most of them involved moving your head to make yourself dizzy on purpose, in order to develop tolerance to dizziness. Very much like an idiot, I shook my head obediently as instructed, from left to right, and up and down.

Feeling dizzy as a result, I left the doctor's office and accidentally made my way to the opposite side of the entrance on the first floor of the clinic, and when I opened the door and went outside, there was a neglected plot of land with weeds growing on it, which looked like the site for a new building. I walked among the weeds, and as I always did when I made a visit to the hospital and learned the cause of my symptoms, I felt both happy and sad to have learned the cause for my dizziness.

And I found something white among the weeds that looked like the backbone of some kind of a vertebrate. It was possible that the thing, which had several joints and looked like the backbone of an animal, wasn't a backbone. Nevertheless, looking at the thing, shining white in the sun, I felt a certain sadness, and felt tempted to make a story out of it, as I'd made a story about false teeth out of a teeth-marked apple sitting on a bench covered in snow in a royal palace in Budapest. But there are some things that are better left alone and kept from developing into a story, which I felt was the case for the thing. Still, I picked up the bone and kept it in a drawer.

For the past several days, in quite a vague state, I spent time making vague or elaborate plans, or making vague plans in an elaborate way, about things I would never do or end up doing. It occurred to me that I was spending each day without any plans as to how I would live in the days to come, with no confidence as to how I would face the very next day, but I thought that it shouldn't be a problem.

Now I'm listening to a monotonic yet strange and beautiful music played on a shamisen. The album was something I bought when I went to Japan after going to the site of the Battle of Waterloo near Brussels, Belgium, where Napoleon's army and the Prussian allies fought a fierce battle—until then, I didn't know that Waterloo was in Belgium, and in the war memorial where there was a room filled with huge panorama pictures (panorama pictures, a forerunner of movies, touch you in a different way than movies, and I feel like a child when I look at them) depicting the war, there was a statement, proudly written, saying that the Belgians devoted themselves to taking care of the wounded on both sides during the Battle of Waterloo, as if that were all that the Belgians, who handed over their land, did—and then returned to Brussels and had a meal at a Japanese restaurant, during which I heard some shamisen music—I ate in the restaurant alone in the afternoon, and the music, monotonous yet intense, touched me in a mysterious way that left an unforgettable impression on me.

Immersing myself in the music, I think that I could write a story with a circular structure in which I somehow extricate myself from the story in which I'm lost and then get lost again entering a story, where my life seems to be.

The story I began to write around the beginning of summer and planned to finish during summer continued into winter, and I seek to end the story as I greet winter, talking about winter in the story. The pumpkin vines in the garden outside the window, which had been thick in summer, and had made a kitten tremble in fear one very bright morning, were nipped by frost and the leaves have withered, but the stems are still intact.

I'm sitting in the sun like a cat. There's nothing but a few withered trees in the garden outside the window. I once had a dream that the landlady of the house I was renting appeared in an empty garden, no, it's possible that it wasn't a garden, but a place I was sure was a garden, or used to be a garden, and suddenly for some reason, took off her pants and paced up and down in her underwear, and then quietly disappeared. No, that's not true. I say that I dreamt it, but it actually happened. I don't know why she did such a thing. Before she went off somewhere, she glanced in the direction of the window where I was, and our gazes met for a very brief moment. I saw two cats playing around at the back, slapping each other with their front paws. It was May then, and there was a thick growth of small leaves that looked like duck feet on the sycamore trees in the garden. The landlady was a bit off in the head, and one day, I saw her walking up and down on a patch of various vegetables on one side of her garden. Once, she brought me an armful of persimmon that I just couldn't eat and

I took them to a nearby woods and wondered what her intention was as I hurled them one by one, counting them—there were twenty-seven in all—but I couldn't be sure.

Generally, a garden is nice to spend time in, and nice to look at through a window. Around the beginning of winter, I went to Brussels for some time to attend a dull literary event, then to Berlin to gauge the publication of a book of mine that was being translated into German (it was fruitless, as expected), and spent most of the time staring at the garden outside the window in a room on the fourth floor of a building that was in a residential area in the city. Being quite dizzy, I had no choice but to stay cooped up in the room most of the time. I had barely managed, in fact, to get to the room in Berlin. I was faced with the greatest crisis at Brussels Airport, when I felt so dizzy after the long flight that I had difficulty just making it to the transfer ramp, so I sat down in a chair with my hands on the cart, and was going to ask someone around me, someone kind looking, to put me in the cart and take me just up to the transfer ramp, but I couldn't bring myself to ask a stranger to do such a thing, and in the end, I made it to the departure gate, pushing the cart and leaning on it, after resting for over an hour.

The only person I knew in Berlin was an old Jewish man who lived in the room next door and who worked as the building manager. He was very old, and had difficulty getting around. We chatted when we ran into each other now and then in the corridor, and I learned that he was from the Czech Republic and spent two years in hiding, seeing almost no light at all, in the home of a kind Christian man, and moved to Israel several years after the war ended, but was unable to settle there because there was something about the place that he didn't like, and returned to live in Germany, and I thought that maybe I could go to Prague when I got better. He told me frankly that he became a little strange after living in a dark, closed space for two years. He was, in fact, receiving ongoing psychotherapy, and had the eyes of someone who was slightly crazy. At a certain time of the day, he listened to some old music on a record that sounded like something that might have been heard playing on the radio during the Second World War, and listening to the sound of the music coming from his room, I could picture him in the dark, listening carefully to the British BBC radio broadcast reporting on the war situation. Still, he looked like someone who was kind by nature, and although he never actually helped me in any way, he tried to help me in one way or another and seemed to regret not being able to help me. I, too, regretted not being able to help him, and it seemed that my regret was greater.

Once when we ran into each other again in the corridor, I wanted to learn more about his past, and he said he'd set aside some time in a few days to tell me. But when the appointed time came and I went to see him in his room, he looked quite unwell, and courteously declined the interview, apologizing that he had been wrong to tell me that he would talk to me. It seemed that he no longer wanted to say anything about his past. I wasn't particularly interested in his past, or the Jewish issue, either, so I said that I hoped he was okay. And when I ran into him again after that, he was doing something astonishing, standing on a small red carpet he'd laid out in the corridor in front of his room and holding some kind of a red flower. He said he was waiting for his boyfriend. But when I returned a couple of hours later after going out, he was still standing in the same spot, holding the flower, looking a little tired and disappointed. But I wasn't sure if he had a lover of the same sex and was waiting for him or if he was doing such a thing because he was out of his mind. It was a sad sight, whether he had a lover of the same sex and had invited him home and was waiting for him, who never showed up, or whether he was doing such a thing because he was off his rocker and imagined up a lover of the same sex who didn't exist. In any case, I hoped that the latter was true, because someone actually being stood up seemed the sadder thing to me. Nevertheless, I pictured him standing before a mirror in his room, holding a red flower on a small red carpet he'd laid out. It seemed like the only thing left for him to do. And it seemed sad but beautiful.

I spent about fifteen days like that, lying on a bed in a room next door to the room of a somewhat strange Jewish man who lived a life similar to that of Anne Frank's at a certain period in time, staring at the garden four floors down, as if staring off into an infinite expanse. For the most part, I didn't really mind that my somewhat poor condition persisted. Sometimes, things were good because I was unwell, and in fact, good ideas often came to me when I was unwell. A poor condition wasn't all bad, at least when it came to writing. But during those fifteen days in Berlin I was in such poor condition that I could do almost nothing. That was an unusual period of time even for me, who had no desire to do anything most of the time, and tried to do as little as possible, as far as I was able to do, or as far as I was able to not do. Unlike at any other period of time I had no desire at all to live, but it wasn't that I was longing to die, either. I was in a very terrible, obscure state in which I didn't want to do anything for myself, and didn't seem to have any strength to do so, either. And I thought as negatively as possible, as if on purpose, although it wasn't on purpose. The thought that I was somehow okay today even in such state, but tomorrow, when tomorrow came, I wouldn't be okay, wouldn't leave me, like some sort of a belief.

All I could manage to do was drag myself out into the street when darkness fell early in the afternoon, and come home after walking on the streets for a little while. And I would return to my room after the short walk, and lie down on the bed and smile faintly in my mind, just managing to feel a pure joy that comes from being drained of all energy. Sometimes the feeling that I was almost perfectly alone, that I had no one, was so appealing that it seemed like something I couldn't give away, not to anyone.

And then I usually took some sleeping pills and fell into a long slumber, like someone who had come to the city in order to sleep. When I woke up, everything seemed so far away, and I felt as if I were in another world different from this one. Sleep, which felt violent yet gentle, seemed like an imaginary creature that gave me a hard time when I came out of it after being in it. I even thought that I could perhaps return to this city someday, only to sleep. My newly prescribed sleeping pills put me in a haze until the next afternoon, and made my palate too sensitive and fussy, making eating, which was difficult to begin with, even more difficult, and had side effects, such as making it so that I couldn't bear the slightest noise, which may have had nothing to do with the sleeping pills because I had always been that way, and perhaps I could learn about other side effects in the future.

But I couldn't fall asleep right away even after taking sleeping pills, and could go to sleep only after a long process of picturing green cats, blue elephants, red cats, yellow hippopotamuses, and so on, or drawing a circle with a chalk on a chalkboard and writing the number 100 in the circle, then erasing the number and the circle with a chalk eraser, and then writing the number backwards.

And whenever I fell asleep in that way, I thought calmly and carefully about the question of taking my own life, as I often do when I become steeped in a sentiment brought on by feelings, and by solitude and thoughts on solitude, that come over me when I'm in a room in a foreign city or other such places. I've thought countless times, of course, about what someone called shy homicide but I considered bold homicide, and the thought of suicide was something that stayed with me, but I didn't come to a decision about it or anything, just as I'd never thought about it before to the point of coming to a decision. And yet I thought once again that I couldn't accept a death of natural causes, that I would end up choosing suicide, a means to end this absurd life in an absurd way, not a final revenge on life, but an ultimate realization of your will. But I couldn't decide on the specific method and time for the execution of suicide. Yet regarding the method, I had a notion that it should be somewhat tragic, but not without dignity—for losing dignity would be the most tragic thing of all. And the time would be at some point in the far or near future, a little before, or much before, the time of my natural death. The time, not specifically appointed, could be appointed in the near future or somewhat far future. So before deciding on the time at which I would go through with suicide, I had to decide on the time at which I would make up my mind about it.

The room I stayed in, thinking such thoughts, wasn't the best place to sleep in, but a moderate amount of noise that created a cozy feeling could be heard from time to time, and although it was cold outside, it was warm inside, and looking at the huge poplar tree in the middle of the garden that looked at least a hundred years old, and was spending the winter in the bone-chilling cold, I felt a sort of satisfaction in that I, at least, wasn't trembling in the cold, and looking at my body, which was as skinny as that of the old Jewish man who lived next door, I thought that my weight remained the same when I almost never ate, but that sometimes, when I ate more than I usually did, I lost weight, but I didn't know the reason why, and wasn't even sure if it was true. And I thought about how once, I had a dream in which I was lying on the floor of a wrecked ship, and things like chairs and drawers and pillows were floating around in the water in the cabin of the wrecked ship, a dream that in itself was like a wrecked ship, and how I thought afterwards that the ship, which sank, unable to bear the weight of my body, would be able to rise above the water only after I disappeared without a trace, or if I sank into a deeper dream, and continuing on with the thought I had in mist-shrouded Venice, I thought about a giraffe that escaped from its cage and was poking its head in through a second story window, opened by someone in the confusion of war or revolution, and continuing with that thought, I thought about lonely declining years made up of days I would start or not start by opening a window, through which a giraffe I was raising would poke its head, and I would pat my cherished giraffe, keenly feeling that the giraffe was all I had left but thinking that it was enough, and of course that was something symbolic, not real, but to me, it was quite real. And continuing on with that thought I thought that perhaps the problem with my life was that for some time now my life has been a full-fledged fight against realism, a fight that was long and difficult, and tedious but pleasant, and felt a vague yet tangible anxiety that the rest of my days may or may not pass in the way I vaguely thought they would, and wondered why I almost never thought about going to the zoo here in Berlin, although when I visited a big city, I always tried, if possible, to go to the zoo that was bound to be there, although that didn't mean that I've been to a lot of zoos, but I couldn't figure out why.

One day, the old Jewish man told me that the poplar was dying of a disease, that nearly all the poplars planted at the center of the countless buildings in Berlin had come down with the disease, and that for some reason, the Berlin authorities were leaving the trees, which were an exotic species, to die. Strangely, the fact that the poplars of Berlin were dying in this way saddened my heart.

Later on, when I was a little better, I took a short walk in the streets around my place from time to time, had a meal, had coffee in a café on the first floor of the building I lived in, then came home. The rest of Berlin seemed too far from me, and it seemed hardly possible for me to go there. At the café, where I became a regular customer after just a few visits, I talked to the café owner, a French man, about Germany and the German people, but mostly he criticized them and I concurred without giving it much thought. He rambled on about how weird and boring the Germans were, and I agreed, saying that in general, people who were weird were interesting, at least, and it was a terrible thing to be just weird, and not interesting at all. And yet he lived in Germany, and had a girlfriend who was German. Regarding that, he said that Berlin, although it was a part of Germany, wasn't like Germany at all, and that his girlfriend also hated the Germans. He said that most of the people living in Berlin were people who hated Germany. According to him, there was no part of Germany, no field or forest, that was untouched by human hands, and the Germans continuously maintained everything in an almost compulsive way, not letting nature stay in its natural state, as if they couldn't condone it. Actually, while traveling in Germany before, I'd felt very uncomfortable, seeing that everything from the fields to the forests was artificial. The French café owner said that in Germany, a country that was like a well-manicured garden in itself, there was no countryside like the French countryside, and that Berlin was the only place in Germany where you could see weeds, and that was the reason why he lived in Berlin. It suddenly occurred to me that the Germans of the past could have made the rash attempt to turn all races into the Aryan race because of some kind of an obsessive compulsive disorder, like the kind that kept them from letting weeds grow anywhere. But thinking about how they tried to make everyone look like them, when they weren't that attractive in general, I thought how ridiculous their scheme was. Even as I sympathized with his expression of antagonism against the Germans, I didn't tell him about the antagonism I'd felt against France while living there.

And one day I ran into a German woman at the café and became friends with her, and we grew somewhat fond of each other, and took a late night walk together from time to time. I thought that she wasn't the type of woman I liked, but I did like her in some ways, perhaps because she was six feet tall, the same height as mine. My feelings for the woman, who looked like a volleyball player even though she wasn't, would have decreased considerably if she was just an inch shorter or taller than I was, I thought (Later, when I learned that she weighed 145 pounds, the same weight as mine, my feelings for her became indescribable). It was an odd criterion for liking someone, but the fact that we were exactly the same, as far as the length of our bodies went, made me like her. To tell the truth, I met, along with her, another woman who was at least six feet tall, and it was this woman who showed more interest in me. To be precise, she showed a little more interest in me than the six feet tall woman did, and I was more attracted to the six feet tall woman.

And for some reason, I really liked the dark green sweater that she, a stage costume designer from the old East Germany who was almost out of work and who, as a result, was almost always free, and was, as a result, very poor, wore, which she knitted herself and was unraveling around the wrist—I thought I could even make love to the sweater—and thought I could keep seeing her as long as she wore the sweater when we met—and during the short time when we saw each other, she continued to wear the sweater when we met, as if she had nothing else to wear. I thought I liked her more because we were the same height and she wore an unraveling sweater, than because of the unique way in which she

spoke English, or talked to another German person, such as a café
employee, in her native German, or sat with her legs crossed, or
twirled her hair as if she were having trouble recalling something.
Looking at her sweater, I would sometimes think, with her sitting
right there in front of me, I'm quite attracted to the owner of that
sweater, what should I do? The sweater was something she made
out of a piece of clothing she bought very cheap at a flea market,
which she cut and sewed up so that the stitching showed on the
outside, and I wandered around the streets with her, who was
wearing the sweater, past midnight, and I was pleased to discover
a ping-pong table in a park near her house where she took me,
because the ping-pong table, which was standing in the middle of
a silent park at two in the morning, looked somewhat out of place.
I thought that two people playing ping-pong, listening to the
quiet sound of a ping-pong ball while other people were asleep,
would make a fine sight, but we didn't play ping-pong or anything.
When we sat down on a bench from which the ping-pong table
could be seen, and she looked at me with her very big eyes and
said, while talking about something, that there was a lake not far
from the park in which people swam in the nude in summer, I
felt an irresistible, fierce desire to pull the unraveling yarn of her
sweater, even if it meant asking for permission, as if that were all
that I wanted in the world at that moment—once, in a similar way,
I was consumed with the desire to pull out at least two or three
of the hairpins in the hair of a woman I met for the first time, for
she was wearing too many hairpins in her hair, thereby ruining
her own hair, and I wanted to help her by pouncing on her and
pulling out her hairpins, in the same way I would want to help

an old woman climbing up the stairs with difficulty (some desires came over me in such violent ways that I had to stand violently against them, or do something by cooperating with them)—and I thought that it might be nice to visit the city again in summer. And at one point her sweater as a whole seemed like a badly tangled skein, and feeling a very strange yet very natural desire to untangle a badly tangled skein, I couldn't resist the desire to pull the unraveling yarn, and told her that, and she graciously said that I could pull it slightly, not too much. I pulled the yarn slightly with caution, and expressed the delight by stamping my feet, and as I did, I thought that there was a certain delight that could be expressed only by stamping your feet. We laughed together, and I felt as if we'd become friends.

When she told me that some time ago, when she was sharing a room with a friend, she was cleaning with the door open, and her friend's robotic vacuum cleaner went out of the house and fell down the stairs, and somehow in the meantime, she found a large black dog standing in the living room, as if the robot cleaner had turned into a dog, I really felt as if we'd become friends. The robot cleaner was stupid and cunningly dodged, as she put it, spots that had to be cleaned, and mostly liked to stay under the bed. And the dog that had suddenly appeared didn't look shabby, but smelled bad as if it had been roaming the streets and sleeping out in the open, so she had no choice but to turn it out of the house, but it wouldn't leave willingly, and in the end, she was able to throw the dog out by turning on the robot cleaner, which she brought back inside, and was fortunately not broken. When she told me that she tried to put a cat she had at the time on the robot cleaner in operation and make it ride around on the cleaner, and finally succeeded after numerous attempts, I told her that she should make the cat ride around on the robot cleaner, wearing a little eye patch, and when she told me that she would, I felt an urge to kiss her. She said that the cat came to enjoy riding around on the robot cleaner very much after that.

And several days later, when we met again in the middle of the night and went to the park, and she suddenly jumped up on the trampoline that was there, and kept bouncing up and down on the trampoline as if overflowing with energy, as if she couldn't control her overflowing energy, she farted unwittingly, without being able to help herself—for she wouldn't have farted on purpose just to let me hear her fart—and when we heard the sound together, I felt an indescribable fondness for her.

The sound of the fart that had come from a woman who was jumping on a trampoline in a silent park in the middle of the night, a woman who was six feet tall, at that, wasn't that loud, and so didn't spread far, far away, cutting through the silence of the park in the middle of the night, but it sounded like the short but clear sound produced by an accidentally disturbed little bell, or the fleeting chirp of a bird, so the incident, which could have been quite embarrassing for both of us, was far from being quite embarrassing for both of us, and became something that made us feel quite merry, before we could even do anything about it. We broke out into merry laughter, and the reason why I felt merry, at least, was because the sound of the fart that had come from a very tall woman I didn't know very well, and vanished into the air, made me think, as it vanished, that it was like a bubble that rose to the surface of a still pond, through a breath exhaled by a fish, or through some kind of an activity at the bottom of the pond. And watching her go up and down in the air on a trampoline in a silent park in the middle of the night, I felt as if she were the last survivor after the extinction of mankind, and jumping on a trampoline seemed just the thing to do for the last survivor after the extinction of mankind. And I thought that if mankind ended up going to a planet other than the moon, on which we have already set foot, the first thing we should do is set up a trampoline there and jump on it. In a way, what the astronaut who took the first step on the moon did was also jump, as if on a trampoline, on the moon whose gravity is much lower than that of the earth—the image seemed to be one of someone leaving his own world and landing on another. I felt an urge to sleep with her, the last survivor of the earth who was jumping on the trampoline by herself after mankind had disappeared. And the urge grew when I recalled that once, while having a meal at a restaurant in mist-shrouded St. Mark's Square, I wondered if there was a trampoline in a park or a playground, with children jumping up and down on it in a thick mist, and thought it would be nice if there were such children.

Physical relations between us seemed a natural thing, only a matter of time, and we both knew that we wanted physical relations, but our relations did not advance into such. For reasons I don't understand, it seems that I anticipated in my heart a development into a physical relationship that could soon take place, but at the same time, wanted to prevent it in any way I could. And there was a practical reason, too, for I wasn't well at the time and wasn't sure if sex was indeed possible. It was almost certain that sex wasn't possible, and I was sure, almost confident, in that respect, and it could be nice to fail in your attempt to have sex with someone for the first time, making that person fail as well, and to do something unforgettable as a man, thus becoming an unforgettable man to that person.

I went to her house that day, but all we did was sit by the window and have a drink. She gave me a seashell as a gift, and told me she collected seashells. But there was only a few shells she'd collected, too few to be called a collection. I told her that I collected bones, and suddenly recalled how, when I went to a snow-covered mountain in Nepal, I tried to find some kind of a bone there as well. I collected bones without thinking that I was collecting them, and there were some animal bones of unknown origin in my house, but not many. Still, I thought that I could collect bones, and that perhaps people could leave their children a certain bone in their body when they died, and that it could be a great keepsake. (And I collected sleeping pills—including tranquilizers and antidepressants—which could amount to a lethal doze when taken at once, but I never thought that I would take them at once someday. I collected leftover sleeping pills as a sort of hobby, just as some people collected things such as stamps or trays or knives. Is this true? Perhaps I'm saying something somewhere between the truth, something close to the truth, and something far from the truth. In any case, I collected a good amount of sleeping pills, with which I filled five small transparent glass bottles, each of which could hold about a hundred pills, and put them in a music box and the kitchen cabinet. The sleeping pills in the cabinet look like a kind of seasoning for food, not medicine. One day, I was so bored that, looking at the glass bottles containing sleeping pills of various colors, I thought I could perhaps crush up the pills to the size of sand grains and create a desert scene of mummies lying in sand, after the manner of sand bottles created by Arab artisans, pouring colored desert sand into glass bottles to reproduce desert scenes, such as oases or camels, to relieve the boredom a little, just a little, really, but I didn't actually do it. But it seemed that doing so would be a kind of little magic, and I was reminded of ancient Arabians, for whom magic was a part of life. A desert scene of mummies lying in sand, made up of grains of sleeping pills that were like sand grains, would enhance the feeling that everything in the scene was in eternal slumber, and be a nice souvenir of my sleeplessness. And I think that one day, I could put a sleeping pill scorpion or palm tree, or fish or dolphin, in a small glass bottle, although it wouldn't be an easy task.) I told her how I used to carry around in my pocket something that looked like a boar canine, which I picked up in a mountain somewhere, and left it in the seat pocket in front of me on a train when I got off. She said that there were a lot of boars living in the forests of Berlin, and that you could see a fox from time to time if you were lucky. I said that if I had a chance, I'd like to go to a forest in Berlin with her to see a fox, but I never got to see a fox in a forest in Berlin. We didn't go to a forest in Berlin together to see a fox, and we didn't meet again, either.

That night, being very passive, I was going to stay the night in her room if she asked me to, but she didn't show that much initiative, thanks to which nothing happened between us. Leaving her house, I thought that I wasn't in a position to be nitpicky, but that I was being strangely fussy, and going down the corridor, I thought that I wanted to keep being fussy.

One day, without a word to her, I moved to a house in another area of Berlin (not far from where David Bowie once stayed), and fingering the very old and chipped seashell I got from the woman who collected seashells, I hoped that the woman, with whom nothing had actually happened, and whom I may be able to suddenly recall in the distant future, after having almost completely forgotten about her, when I saw a woman wearing a sweater, or a child jumping on a trampoline, would be happy, collecting many pretty seashells, and live the life she wanted, and wearing her pretty green sweater, do something similar to farting while jumping on a trampoline in a park in the middle of the night with someone she recently met, making him grow fond of her, and making both of them feel merry, and making them grow affectionate toward each other.

I didn't say anything either to the French owner of the café where I met her, and to be honest, there was nothing to talk about with him besides disparaging things about Germany and the German people. And he was so chatty that I felt like heaving a sigh when I listened to him talk, and all that he said to me were negative things about Germany. On the day I moved, I thought that a virtually nonexistent relationship was all there was to my encounter with her, and felt that my brief encounter with her would remain a good memory for me. And although I wasn't sure if by doing so, I broke the heart of a German woman, and although I didn't think that by doing so, I made a German woman go through what a French girl, who had stood me up long ago, made me go through, but I felt good, thinking that I'd taken some sort of a revenge. I hoped that she, too, would take revenge on someone in the future, if she felt betrayed by me. No, that was a childish, shameful thought, and I tried not to think like that. Could it perhaps be that by doing so, I thought I could figure out the reason why the French girl had stood me up? But I still couldn't figure out the reason. But it wasn't such a bad thing to suddenly recall something that happened with someone because of something that could never be explained, and wonder about it, and still be without an explanation.

In my new area, too, I mostly took brief walks around the house, but most of the time, I stayed in my room. Late at night, I'd go into little parks and playgrounds that made people just pass them by and gave the feeling of being withdrawn, and come to a stop at every street corner as if there were something special there that made me come to a stop even though there wasn't, and roam the building and tree lined streets that gently revealed themselves in the streetlights, with nothing overwhelming about them, and seemed to be giving me their everything and embracing me, and when I did, I felt like a true city walker. And even when I returned to my room after a walk I could see a huge poplar tree in the courtyard, and the moss-covered tree, which didn't really look as if it were dying, looked age old. I spent a lot of time looking at the broken bicycles and strollers discarded around the tree, the way I do when I observe something very carefully, and thought that I was turning into someone or something I'd never considered, and wrote down, in my notebook full of bizarre thoughts, such as, If everything that looks like latex aliens standing next to unstable blue order is heading toward an irrevocable end, there's nothing that can be done about it, and thought about going to a city in Germany someone told me about, with a street whose buildings, from number one to one hundred, were full of offices of one of the greatest publishing groups in the world, and wasn't very much to look at as a city, and also recalled that I once saw, between fields of reeds by a lake created by the only active volcano in Germany, which I visited while traveling long ago in Germany, bubbles that indicated that the volcano was still active. With me at the time was a friend I'd made while traveling somewhere else, a German guy who worked as a stained glass restorer at the Cologne Cathedral, and thanks to him, I had the chance to see a structure at the top of the cathedral that looked like an emptied whale's belly.

Just once I took a night bus in the middle of the night and rode through downtown Berlin to the Brandenburg Gate, the Potsdamer Platz, and the Alexanderplatz, and the snowy streets were almost empty, and the scenes outside the window withdrew like phantoms, and it seemed that during that stretch of time, at least, the silent streets and buildings were the true keepers of the city.

And having returned to my room at dawn, I lay motionless on the bed in the room which had a very high ceiling and imagined that there was a clown with a painted white face on a very long trapeze hanging from the ceiling, the kind you see at a circus, who was sprinkling over me a mysterious white powder that immobilized people, which was why I couldn't move, and that I wouldn't be able to move until I made him fall or dragged him down and immobilized him. In my imagination, the clown was swinging serenely on the trapeze, and already rendered immobile by him, I couldn't find a way to divert his attention from giving me a hard time. If there was such a thing, that is, if the clown had some kind of a weakness, for instance, being afraid of the sound of a cock crowing, I could find it and immobilize him, but I had no way of knowing if he had any kind of a weakness. No, actually, it seemed that I was the one who was making the clown immobilize me. It seemed as if I had in my hand invisible strings attached to the clown's head and arms and legs, and could make the clown move, the way you manipulate puppets, but I couldn't move my hands. In the end, I could move only after making the invisible clown look no longer like a clown, turning him into something that wasn't a clown, and wasn't anything else, either.

But I liked the high ceiling, and felt that I could stay lying down forever if I was under that ceiling. One of the reasons why I almost never left the room was because I loved how high the ceiling was in that room.

But from that room, too, I could see various little movements. Beyond the garden out the window, I could see an old woman walking uncomfortably in the house, with the help of a stick, and a man making something late at night, and strangely, all this made me feel at ease. And through a window of the house to the left of my room, I could see a young woman who lived with a dog. Her dog was very big, and was actually almost as tall as she was when it stood straight up, and sometimes, I could see the dog stand upright on its hind legs and jump at her as if to attack her. I wasn't able to find out what took place between the dog and the woman in her bedroom because of the closed curtains of her bedroom, but I thought, without any real grounds, that the dog was from

Iceland, and even if she had physical relations with a dog, man's best friend, it would be a very natural thing. Anyway, thinking that the garden, through which I could see all this, but which wasn't much to look at in itself, helped me pass such difficult days, fully experiencing the comfort and discomfort brought on by lethargy, I look at the garden in front of my house now, which isn't much to look at, either.

Now winter has passed, and so has spring, and summer has arrived. No, it's not full summer yet, but it's approaching summer. In the meantime (I finished translating *To the Lighthouse,* which ends with the death of some of the Ramsays and the guests who were invited to their home, and with the several who remain taking a boat to the lighthouse) I looked over what I've written, and added some stories and removed others, and corrected what could be corrected, and revised it on the whole. In the process, the story again moved in a direction I wanted or didn't want. And I still haven't put a title to this story, and again, I feel tempted to title it *Vaseline Buddha* or *A Cat Walking on Piano Keys.* But *Untitled* could be a fitting title for this story, which I feel says a lot about a lot of things, but hasn't really said anything at all.

Several days ago, I went out for the first time in a while, because I suddenly wanted to see the dog I named Baudelaire, which looked even more stupid with a tattoo on its eyebrows. But something must have happened to the dog in the meantime, for I never saw it. So I wanted to see the Christian fundamentalist who, standing with a cross in his hand, startled me by shouting loudly when I was walking down the street one day, but I didn't see any such person. But I was startled because a beggar who was sitting on the ground on a street somewhere slapped my leg, and the beggar, a very old woman, asked me for money with desperation on her face, the kind of desperation I hadn't seen in a long time. I glared at her for a moment, upset that she had slapped me, but I was reminded of the woman I'd met in Amsterdam who had spinach stuck between her teeth, and in the end, could come home after giving her some money.

Now there are three cats walking on the roof of the house across the street. I'm not sure if they're the cats I saw walking on the roof last year at the beginning of summer. But cats liked to spend time on the roof, which was sunny, and you could often see a cat, awake from a nap, arching its back all the way and stretching.

Among the cats is one that I saw on a rainy day several days ago, wet and walking in the rain. It's hard to remember the face of a cat that doesn't live with you, but I'd studied the cat's face carefully and remembered it. The cat comes almost every day to the roof of the neighboring house that can be seen out my window, and leaves after taking a nap. We ran into each other a few times in an alley, and every time, the cat glanced at me for a moment and went on its way. One time I was holding an umbrella and I felt as if the cat were looking at me with ridicule, or contempt.

A gray mother cat takes its place on the roof, with a cat that looks like its baby, pretty big but smaller than its mother. I'm not sure if the mother cat is the kitten that had cried painfully, trapped in pumpkin vines, at the beginning of this past summer.

Cats lead a wandering life. No, they lead a roaming life. Perhaps they lead a wandering life, in their own way, as they roam.

Thinking about the roaming or wandering of cats makes me think about wandering again. Anyway, the best travel book of sorts I know, as well as autobiography of sorts, in a broad sense, is Beckett's *Molloy,* and in fact, when I travel, I take *Molloy* with me and read it in my hotel room, or lying in a lounge chair by the pool. But actually, *Molloy* is more of a story about wandering than about traveling, and perhaps one of the greatest misfortunes in the modern times is that the great spiritual human act of wandering has virtually disappeared, and wandering in the true sense is no longer possible. Now, travel is nothing more than an escape from everyday life, which is nothing more than an illusion. And travel is merely an expansion, as well as extension, of everyday life, not really an escape from everyday life. What I actually found during travels undertaken to break free from everyday life was everyday life that was somewhat unfamiliar, or not unfamiliar at all.

Now the cats on the roof are passing the time quietly. A magpie is sitting still on a persimmon tree, and I'm quietly staring at the cats and the magpie. I don't see anything that's vigilantly waiting for an opportunity to do something. There could be some such thing in the pumpkin vines, although I don't see it. The cats and the magpie and I are absorbed in our own worlds, irrelevant to each other. We will stay that way until there's a movement, a noise that catches our attention. After something like that occurs, we will again return to our own worlds and time. Like summer bugs that look like they're flying around heedlessly, or like the bodies of dead stinkbugs or spiders piled up on a windowsill in winter.

In any case, the fact that the cats and the magpie are unaware that I'm writing about them pleases me for no reason. They live in their own worlds. The same is true of myself. And yet they're with me in my imagination and in my story. And I think that I too barely exist in the story I'm writing, and am with myself in the story.

What will I do now that I've written a story? With summer here now I could start writing about the difficulty of passing the summer season, and spend the summer writing.

But for now I don't want to go again into a story, into a deep tunnel.

Instead, I wind the spring of a music box on the table by the window, after the shamisen music comes to an end. I hear music. Like a child, I put words to the music in my mind. But I recite the words, not singing even in my mind, because I hate singing.

> *There's a moving island somewhere in Australia.*
> *And the island continues to move.*
> *The island moves the same distance every year, with the waves moving the sand.*
> *The island remains the same size, with the same amount of sand piling up.*
> *As the island moves, the lighthouse on the island, too, must be moved continuously.*

Thinking about the island, which exists in reality but exists even more vividly in my imagination, I slowly make my way somewhere amid the sound of music. I think it's time to put an end to a long thought.

Thank you all
for your support.
We do this for you,
and could not do
it without you.

DEEP
VELLUM

DEAR READERS,

Deep Vellum Publishing is a 501c3 nonprofit literary arts organization founded in 2013 with the threefold mission to publish international literature in English translation; to foster the art and craft of translation; and to build a more vibrant book culture in Dallas and beyond. We seek out literary works of lasting cultural value that both build bridges with foreign cultures and expand our understanding of what literature is and what meaningful impact literature can have in our lives.

Operating as a nonprofit means that we rely on the generosity of tax-deductible donations from individual donors, cultural organizations, government institutions, and foundations to provide a of our operational budget in addition to book sales. Deep Vellum offers multiple donor levels, including the LIGA DE ORO and the LIGA DEL SIGLO. The generosity of donors at every level allows us to pursue an ambitious growth strategy to connect readers with the best works of literature and increase our understanding of the world. Donors at various levels receive customized benefits for their donations, including books and Deep Vellum merchandise, invitations to special events, and named recognition in each book and on our website.

We also rely on subscriptions from readers like you to provide an invaluable ongoing investment in Deep Vellum that demonstrates a commitment to our editorial vision and mission. Subscribers are the bedrock of our support as we grow the readership for these amazing works of literature from every corner of the world. The more subscribers we have, the more we can demonstrate to potential donors and bookstores alike the diverse support we receive and how we use it to grow our mission in ever-new, ever-innovative ways.

From our offices and event space in the historic cultural district of Deep Ellum in central Dallas, we organize and host literary programming such as author readings, translator workshops, creative writing classes, spoken word performances, and interdisciplinary arts events for writers, translators, and artists from across the world. Our goal is to enrich and connect the world through the power of the written and spoken word, and we have been recognized for our efforts by being named one of the "Five Small Presses Changing the Face of the Industry" by Flavorwire and honored as Dallas's Best Publisher by *D Magazine*.

If you would like to get involved with Deep Vellum as a donor, subscriber, or volunteer, please contact us at deepvellum.org. We would love to hear from you.

Thank you all. Enjoy reading.

Will Evans
Founder & Publisher
Deep Vellum Publishing

LIGA DE ORO ($5,000+)

Anonymous (2)

LIGA DEL SIGLO ($1,000+)

Allred Capital Management

Ben & Sharon Fountain

Judy Pollock

Life in Deep Ellum

Loretta Siciliano

Lori Feathers

Mary Ann Thompson-Frenk
   & Joshua Frenk

Matthew Rittmayer

Meriwether Evans

Pixel and Texel

Nick Storch

Social Venture Partners Dallas

Stephen Bullock

DONORS

Adam Rekerdres

Alan Shockley

Amrit Dhir

Anonymous

Andrew Yorke

Anthony Messenger

Bob Appel

Bob & Katherine Penn

Brandon Childress

Brandon Kennedy

Caroline Casey

Charles Dee Mitchell

Charley Mitcherson

Cheryl Thompson

Christie Tull

Daniel J. Hale

Ed Nawotka

Rev. Elizabeth
   & Neil Moseley

Ester & Matt Harrison

Grace Kenney

Greg McConeghy

Jeff Waxman

JJ Italiano

Justin Childress

Kay Cattarulla

Kelly Falconer

Linda Nell Evans

Lissa Dunlay

Marian Schwartz
   & Reid Minot

Mark Haber

Mary Cline

Maynard Thomson

Michael Reklis

Mike Kaminsky

Mokhtar Ramadan

Nikki & Dennis Gibson

Olga Kislova

Patrick Kukucka

Richard Meyer

Steve Bullock

Suejean Kim

Susan Carp

Susan Ernst

Theater Jones

Tim Perttula

Tony Thomson

SUBSCRIBERS

Aldo Sanchez

Amber Appel

Amrit Dhir

Anandi Rao

Anonymous

Barbara Graettinger

Ben Fountain

Ben Nichols

Benjamin Quasebarth

Bill Fisher

Bob Appel

Brandye Brown

Carol Cheshire

Cheryl Thompson

Chris Sweet

Cory Howard

Courtney Marie

Courtney Sheedy

David Weinberger

Ed Tallent

Frank Merlino

Greg McConeghy

Ines ter Horst

James Tierney

Jeanne Milazzo

Jennifer Marquart

Jeremy Hughes

Jill Kelly

Joe Milazzo

Joel Garza

John Winkelman

Julia Rigsby

Julie Janicke

Justin Childress

Ken Bruce

Kenneth McClain

Kimberly Alexander

Lara Smith

Lissa Dunlay

Lytton Smith

Marcia Lynx Qualey

Margaret Terwey

Martha Gifford

Mary Dibbern

Michael Elliott

Michael Holtmann

Neal Chuang

Nhan Ho

Nick Oxford

Owen Rowe

Patrick Brown

Peter McCambridge

Rainer Schulte

Robert Keefe

Scot Roberts

Shelby Vincent

Steven Kornajcik

Steven Norton

Susan Ernst

Tim Connolly

Tim Kindseth

Todd Mostrog

Tom Bowden

FALL LIST 2016

CARMEN BOULLOSA · *Heavens on Earth*
translated by Shelby Vincent · MEXICO

ANANDA DEVI · *Eve Out of Her Ruins*
translated by Jeffrey Zuckerman · MAURITIUS

JÓN GNARR · *The Outlaw*
translated by Lytton Smith· ICELAND

CLAUDIA SALAZAR JIMÉNEZ · *Blood of the Dawn*
translated by Elizabeth Bryer · PERÚ

JOSEFINE KLOUGART · *On Darkness*
translated by Martin Aitken · DENMARK

SERGIO PITOL · *The Magician of Vienna*
translated by George Henson · MEXICO

EDUARDO RABASA · *A Zero-Sum Game*
translated by Christina MacSweeney · MEXICO

BAE SUAH · *Recitation*
translated by Deborah Smith · SOUTH KOREA